Santa, Baby

A Naughty Christmas Novella

Linda Evermill

Santa, Baby by Linda Evermill

Cover Designer: Linda Evermill

For everyone who ever wanted to sit on a hot Santa's lap...
and loves candy canes just a little *too* much.

Content Warnings

This book contains content that some readers may find distressing.

Trigger Warnings include (but are not limited to):

- Explicit sexual content (Starting page one, I warned you.)
- Consensual kink (light bondage, praise kink, light spanking).
- Grief/loss (past trauma)
- Swearing & adult language
- Immortal x mortal relationship

If you are sensitive to any of these topics, please skip those chapters. Your mental health is the priority.

Playlist

1. Santa Baby – Ariana Grande, Liz Gillies

2. A Nonsense Christmas – Sabrina Carpenter

3. Santa Tell Me – Naughty Version – Ariana Grande

4. Snowman – Sia

5. Cozy Little Christmas – Katy Perry

6. Like Real People Do – Hozier

7. The Walls – Chase Atlantic

8. Mistletoe – Justin Bieber

Five days before Christmas, Santa crashes his sleigh through the roof of a bakery.

Literally.

Nick—Santa Claus—immortal, jaded, and fresh off a little too much fun at the North Pole's end-of-year party. During his drunken joyride, he loses control mid-flight and crash-lands right on top of Sugar & Snow, Everpine's most beloved bakery. The sleigh is wrecked. His reindeer have fled across town.

Stella Grand isn't impressed. She doesn't care that he's Santa.

She. Is. Pissed. They strike a deal: Nick helps Stella operate a holiday pop-up booth for her bakery. Stella helps him hunt down his magical, misbehaving reindeer before Christmas Eve. But the longer they're stuck together—trading insults and smoldering glances—the harder it gets to ignore the heat building between them. Stella might just earn herself a spot right at the top of the naughty list...

And Nick?

He's dying to check it twice.

Table of Contents

Content Warnings..4

Playlist 5

Table of Contents 7

Chapter 1..8

Chapter 2..21

Chapter 3 26

Chapter 4..34

Chapter 5..41

Chapter 6..47

Chapter 7..54

Chapter 8..62

Chapter 9 76

Chapter 10..87

Chapter 11..101

Chapter 12..114

Chapter 13 120

Chapter 14 127

Chapter 15..135

Epilogue 140

Chapter 1

Nick
December 20.

"Oh yes, Nick... fuck!"

Piper's voice was hoarse, echoing off the walls as I pounded into her from behind over my desk. Her fingers clawed at the edge, knuckles white, thighs trembling with every thrust. My cock drove deep, as my hips snapped against her ass with a pace that had nothing to do with love and everything to do with stress relief and end-of-year chaos. She was tight, dripping, and clenching me like she was trying to wring me dry.

"Good little elf," I murmured through gritted teeth, my palm cracking against her ass. She gasped, and her pussy clenched around me again.

A few more thrusts and she was coming, loud and hard beneath me. That was enough to tip me over, too. I spilled inside her with a groan, my grip tightening on her hips as my body vibrated against hers. Snowflakes drifted through the office skylight above, melting on our sweat-slicked skin. The contrast made me shiver, and I dug my fingers deeper into her skin.

Piper sagged forward, catching her breath, a lazy smirk curling her red-stained mouth.

"I have to say," she purred, tossing her purple hair over her shoulder, "your idea of a performance bonus is really motivational."

I tucked myself back into my pants, chuckling. "You earned it. December's hell."

She turned, dragging a nail down my abs. "You're not wrong. But one more week, then vacation."

"Mm," I grunted. "For you, maybe."

She kissed my neck and sauntered off, her hips swaying in a way that made me want to take her again. But, alas, I couldn't. Outside my office, the party was in full meltdown mode.

The end-of-year North Pole bash was chaos incarnate: elves crowding the workshop floor with drinks, tinsel strung from the ceiling, eggnog sloshing everywhere, and someone breakdancing in a Santa hat.

People would assume I get offended by that, but the truth is, I love it, especially since I'm not wearing anything remotely similar. I do have a deep red regular beanie, though. It's nice and warm enough. On that note, why do people assume that I'm an old man with a long beard and a belly? I'm immortal, yes, but I look like a human in his thirties, and as for the belly... My well-worked six-pack would win that argument.

A sleigh bell conga line snaked through the lounge. Vixen's antlers were tangled in a string of LED lights. Someone definitely had too much to drink, because the mailroom elves were grinding to "Jingle Bell Rock."

I fucking hate Christmas music, but for some reason, the elves are going crazy over it, so I let them have it.

Tinker floated next to me, gave me a small pat on the back, and passed me a flask. "Your sleigh's parked, boss, and Dasher's coked out on cinnamon sticks again."

"Perfect," I muttered, swigging hard. The warmth hit my chest, or maybe it was just the rising level of fuck-it energy that had been building since the 1st of December.

I was tired. Not just end-of-season tired. Existentially tired. Eight hundred years of lists and logistics. Chimneys and cookies. People don't believe anymore. Magic's different now, louder and harder to steer. People would assume my life is full of joy and magic, but the truth is, it gets lonely. Sure, I have my elves to keep me company, and don't get me wrong, burying myself deep in Piper does make me joyful. , but it's just that and no more. And to be honest, I never really wanted more; however, it does get lonely. I wasn't even sure what more was in my case.

And at that moment, the only thing that kept me from snapping was the way Tinker was looking at me.

I could've rested, but the party felt too good and alive for me to leave it. After this, we would only have the headache until the 25th. And I would've been damned if I missed any second of it.

So I did what felt like the only reasonable decision left: I drank shots from Tinker's belly button.

She giggled as I hauled her up onto one of the workshop tables, knocking over a tray of half-built toy trains. Elves hooted and cheered around us, but I barely noticed. I was too focused on the shimmer in her eyes and the way she arched under my touch. I poured the shot onto the dip of her stomach. She shivered when the liquid hit her skin.

"Be good, Tinker," I murmured, leaning in close, breathing warm against her navel. "Don't make me spill it."

She squirmed, muscles twitching as I dragged my tongue slowly across her skin, chasing the liquor. She moaned, and I felt the tension in her body melt under my mouth.

I sucked the shot from her belly button, hot and slow, savoring the burn as it slid down my throat. A deep heat spread through my veins, and a familiar numbness started to take over.

Tinker was already grinning, flushed and wild-eyed.

"My turn," she purred, and pushed me back with a firm hand.

I let her, of course. She climbed on top of me, straddling my hips right there on the table, and poured the next shot into the hollow of my chest. Her tongue felt wicked on my skin, and as the alcohol settled in me, the world around me blurred.

"Ride! Ride! Ride!" The elves chanted as I grabbed the reins and stumbled toward the sleigh.

It gleamed under the night sky, cherry red and golden, runes etched into the leather harnesses. Nine restless reindeer lined up in front of it, who pawed at the ground like racehorses on steroids. The snow was falling thick around us, and the sky was full of stars.

"Okay..." *hiccup.* "Okay." I raised my hands, and the crowd quieted. "Let me show you how it's done."

"Nick...," Piper leaned out from the back of the crowd, her voice tight with concern.

I waved her off. "Just a quick loop, Pipes. Gotta give the people what they want, right?"

I hauled myself into the sleigh, not as smoothly as usual, but I made it.

"Nick, you're drunk," Piper warned me again.

I tightened the reins in my hand. "I know, I know, *Don't Drink and Drive.* But that doesn't apply to magical vehicles."

"What do you mean? It applies especially to magical vehicles!" Piper squeaked, but I snapped the reins.

The sleigh lunged into the sky, faster than I could brace for. My stomach lurched as the wind slapped me in the face. The rush of magic settled on my tongue, and finally, nothing held me down. I took another swig from the bottle tucked against my chest.

"I'm motherfucking Santa! Woooooo!" I screamed into the sky when the sleigh veered hard to the left.

Dasher bucked, Blitzen kicked back, and Vixen growled like he'd had it with me. The sled jerked and dipped low as the harness twisted in my hand.

"Whoa, easy!" I shouted, yanking the reins.

Too late. They weren't listening to me, and I was too buzzed to control them.

Below me, a small town glowed in the snow, white lights, tin roofs, Christmas trees in every window. Like a fricking postcard come to life.

The reins slipped through my hand, and despite my warning, the reindeer wouldn't listen to me. The wind tossed the sleigh, and it took everything I had not to vomit everywhere.

Hmm. And one building certainly was getting closer. I guess it looked like a bakery?

Wait... why is it getting closer?

No. Nope. Shit.

BOOM.

My ears were ringing, and I barely had time to register what had just happened. My reindeer scattered like the wind. I reached for Vixen, but he snorted and leaped over me like he was flipping me off with his hooves. I heard bells jingling off in the woods, and a very familiar "fuck you" snort from Comet.

"Well, that's not ideal."

The sleigh groaned as it slid off the roof and crashed into the snowy backyard below in a pile of glitter, cracked shingles, and shame. The roof was destroyed, with pieces flying everywhere.

A door slammed open with brute force.

Okay. *Showtime.* I just had to make the owner a little starstruck so they wouldn't get *that* mad. I managed to scramble onto my feet as the world slightly tilted around me.

Alright... bakery owner, get ready for the best Santa impression you've ever seen.

"Ho-ho-ho... fuck."

My stomach lurched, and my gaze landed on the owner, who looked like she was trying to shoot daggers with her eyes. She was five feet six of holiday fury in a Christmas-themed pajama set. Her ginger braid was a mess, her cheeks flushed and dotted with small freckles, her eyes green and glittering with rage.

"WHAT THE HELL?!"

I raised a finger, squinting at her. "I know what you're thinking..." *hiccup.* "Santa? Real? It's okay, baby."

Her brows furrowed, and she somehow looked even more furious. *How the fuck do I diffuse this bomb?*

She glared at me with her fists clenched. "You've got *three seconds* to explain why my entire prep kitchen is covered in jingle balls."

I blinked. "But I..." I just gestured to my face and sleigh, and then the sky.

She folded her arms. "You're Santa. Cool. Got it. Still don't give a single fuck. You DESTROYED my shop FIVE DAYS BEFORE CHRISTMAS."

I know I wasn't supposed to be thinking about fucking at that moment, but damn it, she was so cute when her cheeks reddened as she shouted at me.

Focus, Nick.

"Wait..." *hiccup.* "Do you live in a bakery?"

"I live in the house behind the bakery." She said her fists clenched tight beside her.

"Well, you should really make the roof Santa-friendly."
The world swirled around me as I tried to maintain my
balance.

She narrowed her eyes. "You drunk?"

"Festively impaired," I corrected.

She lunged at me.

I dodged, caught her wrist mid-swing, and for a second
we froze. Her chest brushed mine, and electricity hummed
between us. She smelled like cinnamon, and warmth spread
through my chest.

"Name's Nick," I murmured. "And you are...?"

"Pissed. Off."

"Beautiful name."

She glared. "You wrecked my shop!"

"I know how to make an impression."

"Do you have a concussion?"

"No, but thank you for checking. Got a boyfriend,
gorgeous?"

"I should call the cops," She huffed.

I stepped closer, voice dropping. "You're welcome to. But I doubt they know how to trap magical reindeer. And judging by the bells I just heard, nine of them are running wild through... What's this place called?"

"Everpine." She hissed, her face starting to resemble a tomato soup. "Wait...what? Reindeer?"

I pointed up through the hole in the roof. "They panicked. Took off."

We stared at each other like it was some kind of standoff.

"Just fix my roof!" she stomped like a child, though still managed to do it with grace.

"Help me find them, Sweetheart," I offered, "and I'll rebuild your roof."

"Oh no, I don't owe you anything," she crossed her arms, defiance burning in her eyes.

Oh, I love a brat.

I stumbled forward a few steps. "That's true, but if I don't have my reindeer, I can't leave. I'll stay here... with you." I smirked, and it didn't sound like a bad idea.

"Fine," she said, voice sharp. "Start with the roof. And if you call me Sweetheart again, I'll frost your balls."

I grinned, slow and wicked. "Kinky."

"GET. TO. WORK." Her cheeks flared again. I managed to take a few more steps before the world tilted around me. Darkness crept at the edge of my vision.

Huh, I guess I'm drunker than I thought.

Chapter 2

Stella
December 20.

He passed out. I had a passed-out Santa in my garden.

Fuck. My. Life.

"Merry fucking Christmas to me," I muttered, grabbing his arm.

He was heavy. Like in a big, solid, *irritatingly sculpted* kind of way. He smelled like firewood, bourbon, and a hint of sugar, which frankly, felt like a personal attack.

Eventually, with enough swearing to get me banned from three churches, I dragged him back to my house, through the sliding door, and into the storage room that doubled as my office-slash-lounge. I shoved a sack of flour out of the way and dumped him onto the beat-up leather couch.

He sprawled like he owned the place. One arm was thrown over his head, mouth slightly open. Smug, even in sleep. With a huff, I allowed myself one moment to really take a good look at him.

His tanned skin was inked with snowflakes and Norse-looking runes. A scar curved just under his ribcage, old, white, and jagged. His sweater had been half-ripped off during the crash, exposing too much. Way too much. No one that annoying had any business being that hot.

But it wasn't just that. It was the absurdity of it all.

The wreckage. The sleigh. The *actual reindeer* hoof prints are outside. And now this man, this tall, drunk, muscled myth, was snoring on my couch like he hadn't just totaled my roof and crash-landed through my life.

Santa Claus. Real. Apparently.

Maybe I'm still asleep. Maybe I hallucinated the whole thing. Perhaps I'm in a coma from stress, and this is some weird, horny holiday fever dream. That would explain a lot.

The couch groaned under his weight. I watched him for one more second, to make sure he wasn't going to roll over and die or, worse, wake up and flirt with me again.

Then I turned away and pushed through the doors, back into the wreckage of my kitchen.

FUCK.

My prep station was buried under collapsed ceiling beams. I clutched the edge of the counter, trying not to cry.

Five days.

That was all I had until Christmas Eve. My busiest week. The one I depended on to pay my rent through spring. Tourists. Locals. I'd prepped for weeks, dough frozen, fillings bagged.

And now?

Now I had a hole in my roof the size of a minivan, a half-naked myth passed out on my office couch, and nine magical reindeer scattering holiday chaos across Everpine.

I wanted to scream.

Instead, I grabbed a trash bag and a flashlight. Dawn was coming, slow and pink, glinting off the snow piled in my prep room, and when the sun rose, so would my customers. People who expected cinnamon rolls and bourbon-laced cocoa and cardamom snowflakes.

I needed a plan. Since His Winter Highness had passed out, he couldn't fix my roof. But I couldn't afford to close. Not a chance.

If I didn't open, people would talk.

If I looked closed, they wouldn't come back.

If I *looked* fine, maybe I could buy myself a little time.

This bakery was my dream. The one thing that kept me going after the fire in Boston. I couldn't lose it because of this. I wouldn't lose it because of this.

I shoveled broken glass into a trash bag. I scooped up anything salvageable and wiped surfaces. I swore a lot in the process, but at least it kept me sane. I repositioned tables to hide the worst of the wreckage. The storefront was mostly intact, thank God. Some glass cracked in the door, and a few displays had toppled, but the register still worked. The espresso machine was mercifully untouched.

But still, it wasn't enough. People couldn't sit down, and what was worse, all the appliances in the prep kitchen were ruined.

I moved some furniture around, aligning them into circles in front of the store. Dragged a huge-ass table outside, and I chalked up a message with stiff fingers:

SUGAR & SNOW

Pop-Up Opens Today!

Cocoa | Cookies | Christmas Chaos

I paused, glancing back through the doorway. Nick, Santa, whatever, was still asleep, sprawled like a Renaissance painting.

I turned back to the counter, tied on a fresh apron, and whispered to myself like a prayer:

"This will work. You are not losing this bakery to Christmas bullshit."

Chapter 3
Stella
December 21

By the time the sun cleared the pines, I'd worked my ass off and lied my ass off to everyone who walked past the store, gawking and gasping.

"It's alright, just a little... *renovation*." I plastered a smile that felt unnatural. "Worry not, folks, Sugar & Snow is still open, and spoils you with treats."

The kitchen, behind the storefront, my personal kitchen, miraculously survived. Cramped, but it was functional. Which meant I could still bake. Just... slower. Smaller batches. No prep kitchen, no extra ovens.

The plan was relatively easy.

Bake like hell in the back. Dash to the booth when I heard the little bell on the stand jingle.

Smile. Sell. Run back in. Repeat.

Exhausting? Yes.

Possible? Maybe.

Better than closing for five days? Absolutely.

Maggie would never forgive me for that. She was the kind of mentor who lived for work, and she taught me that too. I wasn't as much of a workaholic as she was, but it was a great motivational tool to think about her at times like this.

I was halfway through rolling out cinnamon dough when I heard him groaning in the back room. I wiped my hands on my apron, then stormed in, my heart already pounding. He was awake. Bleary-eyed, half-dressed, hair a mess of silver curls, blinking at the couch like it personally betrayed him, for not being his bed.

"Well, good morning, Claus," I deadpanned. "How's the hangover?"

"Oh, shit," he muttered. "You still look angry."

"Oh, do I?" I smiled sweetly. It was anything but kind. "Maybe that's because you crashed through my ceiling and destroyed my busiest week of the year."

He scrubbed a hand down his face, then looked around, confused. "Wait... did you... Did you carry me in here?"

27

I crossed my arms. "Dragged. Dropped you on your head a few times for good measure."

A rough laugh escaped him. "I can feel that."

I tossed him a pile of folded clothes I had asked my neighbor for. "Get dressed, Santa. You've got work to do."

He took the bundle, hooked the ruined sweater casually over one shoulder, and then just stood there, half-naked, chest bare and glistening with leftover glitter from who-the-fuck-knows what.

Runes inked across his ribs. A light dusting of silver hair across a *ridiculously* firm chest.

Unfair.

He belonged on a romance novel cover, not wrecking my bakery and flashing me his... sleigh bells.

I worked down a swallow and tried not to stare. He saw it. Of course he did. His lips curled into a smirk, one that made the heat crawl up my neck.

"See anything you like?"

How can someone be this much of an asshole?

"I would rather drown in flour." I clipped out, somehow managing to keep my voice steady. "Besides, I don't want to catch some kind of elf STD."

Nick laughed, like a proper fucking belly laugh. "Elf STD?"

I crossed my arms and nodded, even though I sounded ridiculous.

"Mmh-hmm," he murmured. "Okay, well, I should probably go find my reindeer..."

"Wrong," I snapped, slamming the door open behind me. "You need to help me right now, because I've got a line of customers outside and I can't bake and sell at the same time. And since you passed out and didn't fix my roof, you need to be my cashier."

"Alright-Alright, Sweetheart." He said, holding up his hands in defense.

"My name is Stella, not Sweetheart. Let's go."

By the time Nick sauntered out front, I was already two trays deep into my second batch of cinnamon snowflakes and was running on caffeine and rage. Well, mostly on rage.

He walked up like he owned the place, shirt half-buttoned, sleeves pushed to his forearms, that damn smirk playing on his lips like he's doing *me* a favor just by breathing the same air.

I watched from the kitchen window as he stepped behind the booth. The man had never used a cash register in his life, and it was obvious from the way he scratched his head.

I ran up to him and quickly gave a 'How to Use the Register 101.' Then, of course, I paced back to the kitchen just in time before the snowflakes burned.

"Don't break anything," I called out through the propped door, juggling the hot trays.

He didn't even look back. Just waved a hand. "Relax, boss. I'm great with people."

His first customer approached, a middle-aged woman in a velvet reindeer hat. She peered at the menu chalkboard with exaggerated delight.

Nick flashed her a thousand-watt grin. "What can I get you, darling?"

She giggled. GIGGLED.

She was old enough to be his grandmother. Well, maybe that's not true. Nick could probably be old enough to be her great-great-great-great-great-grandfather.

"Oh my," she said. "Are you new here? Stella's never had someone so... festive at the booth before."

He leaned in like he was telling a secret. "Seasonal hire. Just helping out while the bakery gets... *redecorated*."

She blushed. "Well, aren't you sweet?"

"I'm a lot of things," he purred. "Sweet is just the first layer."

Jesus Christ.

I nearly dropped the tray in my hand. He rang her up for two cardamom snowflakes and a cocoa, then turned toward the door, showing me a thumbs-up. I rolled my eyes and willed myself not to smite him in front of everyone.

The line was growing. People were trickling in, attracted to the smell, the music, and *the man-shaped magnet with a beard* behind the booth. I could hear his voice; he was laughing, teasing, and charming every damn person who walked up like he'd been running holiday pop-ups his whole life.

I passed him an order through the window. He winked. "Thanks, Sweetheart."

"Remember what I said, what happens if you call me Sweetheart?" I cocked an eyebrow, trying really hard not to lose my cool.

"You wanna do it now, sweetheart?" he teased, and I groaned, rolling my eyes.

I was starting to get concerned for my eyes, because ever since he appeared, I'd been rolling them so much it was probably unhealthy.

Nick strolled casually back to the booth, sweet-talking to all the customers. It was actually frustrating how good he was with people, and from this angle, I could see how he was Santa. From every other angle, he was more like the Devil.

"Is that your boyfriend?"

The question cut through the clatter. A teenage girl, probably from high school, pointed at Nick as he leaned against the booth, licking cocoa foam off his thumb.

What the fuck is he doing? That cocoa was for a CUSTOMER.

My heart stuttered as I pushed open the door. "Absolutely not."

"He looks sooo dreamy." The girl swooned, and I hated that it bothered me.

"Oh, don't let the looks fool you." I snorted, "GET BACK TO WORK!" I shouted to Nick to distract myself.

He saluted with the cocoa cup. "Yes, boss."

I might as well tell everyone Christmas will be canceled this year, because I'm going to kill Santa Claus.

Chapter 4
Stella
December 21.

The booth wasn't a disaster as I had imagined it. Of course... maybe it was thanks to the asshole with the natural holiday glee.

Fuck. Him.

Nick was far too good at smiling at strangers, charming old ladies, and making parents laugh while handing sugar cookies to their kids like he didn't drunkenly crash through my roof *less than twenty-four hours ago.*

Santa Claus, my ass. He shouldn't look like that. The man is full of muscle, and he evaporates sexual energy from all his pores. Nobody who eats that many cookies should have *abs.*

Every time he lifted a tray, the hem of his borrowed shirt rode up, flashing a line of inked skin and muscle so defined, I wanted to smack him with a rolling pin.

Was I horny? Probably.

Was I furious? Absolutely.

Was this healthy? ... Let's not dig too deep.

We were packing up the booth around 7 p.m. Most people had drifted off to the Christmas market and the skating rink. I was just about to yell at Nick for stacking my dishes like a psychopath when...

Jingle. Jingle.

What the fuck?

"Is that...?" I asked, raising an eyebrow.

He nodded, wiping his hands in his black jeans, and started moving slowly towards the door. "Sure is, Sweetheart."

I followed him down the steps, arms crossed. "Call me that again, and I will stick a candy cane so far up your..."

"Shh." He said, holding up his hand.

We stopped in our tracks a few yards from the bakery. Across the street, at the entrance to Everpine Park, the nativity display stood silent. Baby Jesus. Hay bales. The three kings. No tourists around. Empty.

Except... not.

A black blur darted behind the hay bale. Antlers caught the light.

Nick's eyes widened. "Dasher. Little bastard." He took off running.

"Wait... what?" I sprinted after him, apron flapping, boots crunching snow.

What followed could only be described as *reindeer parkour.*

Dasher leapt over baby Jesus like an Olympic gymnast, ducked under the halo of an angel cutout, and darted toward the trees. Nick bolted after him, yelling like a lunatic. I followed, panting.

"DASHER!" Nick shouted, but Dasher flipped him off with his tail.

I was wheezing. "Okay, but... I love him."

"He mocks me," Nick grumbled. "He's the fastest. And he *knows* it."

I spotted a string of Christmas lights still plugged in, running low across the trees. "Can we lasso him?"

Nick's grin returned. "You're a genius."

"Oh, please tell me something I don't know."

We looped the lights, crept around the park perimeter, and spotted Dasher sniffing at a reindeer display, confusion in his eyes. He paused when he saw us. We locked eyes, the tension hung thick in the air, then he huffed and bolted. I dove, tackling him mid-leap. We tumbled into a snowbank, me, Dasher, and then Nick, who crashed on top of us, laughing his stupid, *sexy Santa laugh*.

"Well, damn," he breathed, panting above me. "You're stronger than you look."

"I did carry your stupid ass inside. Did you forget?" I asked, wrestling with him AND Dasher.

He tilted his head with a smug grin. I glared up at him, snow clinging to my lashes, my breath fogging the space between us. His lips were inches from mine. The way his breath mingled with mine made my pulse race. There was a pull in my chest strong enough, almost to make me forget that I hated him.

It would be so easy to get just a little taste...

Of course, that's when Dasher sneezed in my face and tried to bolt again.

Nick collapsed beside me in the snow, laughing so hard he choked. I sat up, wiping reindeer snot from my cheek and summoning every ounce of willpower not to scream into the sky.

While laughing his balls off at my misfortune, Nick managed to catch Dasher before he could go far.

He conjured some cuffs from thin air and slapped them onto Dasher.

"What are those?" I asked, between *gagging*.

"These," he tightened the cuffs, "are making sure the little troublemaker can't leave."

Dasher huffed in disagreement, but let himself be dragged back to the backyard of the bakery.

I hurried into the house, grabbed towels, and desperately tried to clean myself. Every inch of me was covered in snot, so I shed my clothes in the middle of my office and put them in a pile. A pile I was definitely going to light on fire later.

For a moment, I stood there completely naked and my chest heaving with rage. I had used at least three towels to feel somewhat close to clean enough to step into the shower and the rest of my house.

I froze when I heard a low whistle behind me. I could barely force myself to glance back, but when I did, Nick's grin was already there.

"Looking hot, Sweetheart," he said, his gaze dropping to my bare ass, and my cheeks flared, and my thighs clenched.

"Oh my God, get out!"

Nick's amused laugh bounced off the walls. "Hey, it's okay. Own that you're hot, like I do." he shrugged while I desperately tried to cover myself with dish towels.

"You're not the one who's naked." I hissed.

Something sparkled in his eyes, like pure mischief. "That can be easily fixed."

Before I even had a chance to mutter out some response, he was stripping down naked at record speed. My mouth went dry as I stood there, shocked. His inked muscles stretching before me, those muscular thighs and that big and thick co...

No. Nope.

I was going to ignore the pulsating between my legs.

"You're insane," I mumbled, trying to hide the flush rising in my cheeks.

"Ah, but it seems like you like it," he said, his gaze dropping to my breasts, where one nipple poked through the dish towels.

My whole body shook, but I wasn't sure if it was from anger or because I suddenly *really* wanted to be alone with my shower head.

"I'm going to take a shower, and *you* can clean up your mess," I said, motioning towards the roof.

"So you don't want me to join?" he asked, wiggling his brows.

"No." I clipped, pushing past him. "Four days," I muttered to myself, but he heard me.

He caught my arms, turning me towards him. "Plenty of time."

Chapter 5
Stella
December 22 - night

After a very thorough shower and a few intense solo orgasms (thanks, shower head), where I definitely did not think about that thick Santa cock, I passed out in my bed.

I just kept thinking about Nick and the mess, the bakery, and the fire, and my body finally gave up.

Around 1 a.m., I woke up to the sound of hammering and cursing. With a groan, I jumped out of bed.

What fresh hell is this?

Maybe the Easter Bunny crashed into my shop as well. I could have a complete set of magical creatures by New Year's Eve.

I wrapped myself in a cardigan and rushed outside, preparing for the worst. Nick was up on the roof, muttering curses, trying to install a tarp over the hole.

A sigh of relief left me when I saw that he didn't make matters worse. But what the fuck was he doing?

I folded my arms. "Is this your version of fixing things?"

He froze mid-knot, then peered over the edge, his silver hair caught in the moonlight. A smug grin tugged at the corner of his mouth. "Improvising."

"Get down before you hurt yourself," I shouted. I had so had it with him.

"I'm immortal, sweetheart."

I was too tired to complain about the nickname again. Honestly? It was kind of growing on me.

"Okay, don't get mad," Nick said, and he hopped off the roof. Not climbed. Just sort of... glided, like the rules of gravity didn't apply to him.

"Oh, this is a great start," I arms folding tight across my chest.

He actually looked at me... sheepish. "I know it's not great. But I didn't want the snow to get in. Figured a tarp's better than nothing."

I snorted. "Can't you just... You know Santa magic *zip-zap*? Like you did with those scuffs?"

I felt hilarious. There's a sentence you don't say every day. Or every lifetime.

Nick rubbed the back of his neck. "Kinda. I've got some juice left." He lifted a hand, conjuring a flickering gold spark between his fingers. "Small stuff? No problem. I can easily summon small items and sprinkle some magic here and there."

My brows knitted together. "*Okaaaay*, then conjure a new roof."

He sighed. "Big spells like that require the true juice. The real power. That's back at the Pole. Without the sleigh and more importantly, without my reindeer, I can't go back. I'm stuck."

"What?! You said you'd fix my roof!" I squeaked, then realized it was the middle of the night and I could wake up the whole neighborhood.

"I thought I could get back to the North Pole faster. I really am sorry." Nick said, dropping his gaze.

I stared at the poorly installed tarp. The wind flapped it, and somehow it was both comical and sad.

"Okay, so no roof fixing for me before Christmas, I guess," I muttered, and I couldn't hide the disappointment that crept into my voice. I crossed my arms tighter, while I imagined the worst-case scenarios, if my roof didn't get fixed.

His expression softened with honest regret. This time, there was no bullshit in his eyes. I tried to stand my ground. But fuck he was tall and handsome, and somehow warmth radiated from his body even through the cold.

"Look," he searched for my gaze. "I know I've been an ass, and I ruined your shop at the busiest time of the year."

I softened my gaze, but I didn't answer, just stared at him. The fight in me wavered. Not because he didn't deserve my simmering rage, but because even if he made a shitty tarp, he still tried to do something.

"I promise you, Sweetheart," he added, "the second I get back to the North Pole and recharge, fixing your roof will be my priority."

The sincerity in his voice loosened something in my chest. My shoulders relaxed slightly. It was not forgiveness, but it was a pause. A softening. Maybe a truce?

"Until then," he said, tilting his head, "I'll help you every day. The booth, the baking, the cleanup, whatever you need. I owe you."

I chewed on my bottom lip for a second before muttering, "Damn right you do."

He smiled, not with his usual smugness this time, but that only lasted for a second.

"Wanna shake on it?" he asked, extending his hand.

Something was seriously wrong with me, because just the idea of touching him sent a traitorous jolt of electricity straight to my clit. Which frankly was rude of my body, because, newsflash, he was an arrogant, annoying, shirtless disaster.

Composing myself, I arched a brow. "Are you trying to get me to touch you?"

He lifted both hands in mock innocence, like I hadn't caught him thinking inappropriate thoughts every five minutes. "Sweetheart, I have a loooot of ways to get you to touch me."

I snorted. "In your dreams, Claus."

He wiggled his eyebrows. "Is that a promise?"

I scooped some snow in my hand and tossed a snowball at him. It hit his chest with a satisfying *thwack*.

"Get the fuck inside," I muttered, turning on my heel. "I need to sleep before I murder you."

I stomped towards the house, heart pounding for many reasons. I could hear him laughing behind me, and somehow, the sound followed me even in my dreams.

Chapter 6

Nick

December 22

I woke up stupid early. Stella was still asleep, curled up in a tangle of blankets that looked way too cozy for her own good.

I stretched, cracked my back, and slipped out for a quiet stroll around Everpine. The snow crunched beneath my boots, and the whole town still felt like it was dreaming. I almost forgot what it was like to be with humans.

And Stella... she was a special kind of trouble. I'm not usually the guy who wallows in guilt, but she had me rethinking a few things. She was beautiful, sure, her body was to die for, but that wasn't the thing that truly wrecked me. She was stunning where it actually mattered, on the inside. The fire in her, the determination, she was really someone who could handle me. If...

What? No. I can't believe I am actually thinking about dating, and, nonetheless, dating a human. I can't be that desperate for connection.

But she's not just any human.

The thought pierced through me. And I shook my head to usher it away. *She's not just any human; she's my Stella.*

No, Nick, stop. You've known her for a day and a half.

You know you can feel that she is your...

Yanking my thoughts away, I finally heard the telltale sound, sharp, bright, and unmistakable.

Jingle.

My head snapped up. I turned slowly, scanning the tree line. And there, just near the corner of the bookstore, I spotted a flicker of movement. Antlers. A shimmer of magic.

Cupid.

He saw me and instantly froze. I swear, I could see the gears turning behind those big glittery eyes. He was already plotting.

"Don't you dare, Cupid," I raised my voice and took a cautious step forward.

He wiggled his nose, clearly unimpressed by my attempt.

"Dasher is already back at the house. I know how much you love him."

One step closer, he didn't move. He snorted as he could see through my crap, but when I conjured up the cuffs, he let me lock them on. We walked back together, him huffing every few steps like I've personally offended him. Which, I probably had.

When I got back, Stella was still asleep, so I brewed some coffee and glanced at her menu. I didn't know much about baking, but I figured I could manage a few cookies, right?

Wrong.

By the time she woke up, the small kitchen looked like a bakery crime scene, and she looked absolutely horrified.

Her eyes were still puffy with sleep as she took in the scene: me, covered in flour, standing in what looked like the aftermath of a sugar tornado. Frosting on the counters.

Dough stuck to the ceiling. A mixing bowl steaming ominously on the stove.

"Good morning." My try at being nonchalant went down the drain.

"What. The. Fuck. Did you do?!"

She was awake now, storming towards me.

I rubbed the back of my head, spreading even more flour into my hair. "I wanted to help."

"By wrecking what little I have left of my kitchen?"

"Hey," I said, holding up my hands, "I usually eat the cookies, not make them."

For a moment, I truly believed she might hit me or explode from anger when I added.

"I caught Cupid."

She stopped looking at me, confused. "Who?"

"Another reindeer. Only seven more to go, yay," I added jazz hands and hoped to distract her from the mess.

"Get out of my kitchen and set up the booth outside," she hissed in a tone I wouldn't dare to argue.

"Yes, ma'am." I hurried outside, and I behaved like a good little Santa all morning.

By the afternoon, business was booming, and Stella managed to salvage the kitchen disaster.

The line was growing, and she was in overdrive mode, while I managed to charm everyone so well that they didn't even mind the wait.

By the time we closed at seven, Stella looked like a giant gingerbread with all the frosting and flour covering her. She looked exhausted, and I couldn't help but feel guilty.

This is my fault after all. I wanted to do something nice for her, something that wouldn't turn out to be a disaster like baking.

"Get cleaned up and get dressed. I'm taking you out," I grinned, but she didn't look convinced.

"Absolutely not. I want a bath and sleep."

I rolled my eyes while pushing her towards the bathroom. "Do as you're told, Sweetheart."

She snapped, and it was so fucking cute. "You know I'm not your pet to give me nicknames, right?"

I dropped my voice low, and I couldn't hide the mischief beaming in my eyes. "So, what you're saying is that you would be opposed to being my pet?"

She froze, her cheeks flushed.

"... Yes." Her voice pitched at the end of the word like it was a question.

"Are you asking?" I stepped closer, loving the way her chest heaved. Fuck I wanted to touch her.

I knew that I had been teasing since I arrived, but the more time I spent with her, the more I felt like the fire inside her wrapped around me. She was so determined, and she didn't fall for my bullshit. She didn't even care that I'm Santa - freaking - Claus.

Warmth sparked in my chest as I looked her up and down, and a strange tug in my chest begged me to drag my tongue over every inch of her body. But it wasn't just that, and that scared me the most. I didn't want to touch her just physically. I wanted to be with her, spend time with her, and get to know her.

She groaned and turned on her heel. "Fine, I'll go out with you."

Chapter 7
Nick
December 22.

Okay, so I was nervous. I changed my shirt like three times, which was the number of shirts I had, which were not mine but the ones Stella borrowed from one of her neighbors.

I didn't know why I was acting like this was a date. It wasn't. Was it? It shouldn't be. I shouldn't be thinking about her like this, not when I know this can't go anywhere. I can't stay, and she can't exactly come live in the North Pole. We'd have the world's most catastrophic long-distance relationship.

Still, I couldn't stop the warmth crawling up my chest at the thought that maybe this was a date.

Stella stomped out of her room, wearing a short black coat. Tight wine-colored dress that hugged her hips in a way I'd be thinking about for the rest of my immortal life. Black tights. Ankle boots. Her braid was neater than usual, a little makeup dusted on, just enough to make her lips look kissable, and her cheeks look warm.

"Quit staring," She said flatly while she grabbed a purse.

"I can't," I replied, because I had no shame and no ability to lie when she looked like that. Truth be told, I could look at her all day, hair messy, hands dusted in flour, eyes full of fire.

She rolled her eyes but didn't stop me from offering my arm. Her fingers slid into the crook of my elbow, and I swear I felt the temperature spike around us. Or maybe that was just my blood boiling.

We walked down Everpine's cobbled street, all string lights and garland and perfect snow. It should've been cheesy. It wasn't. It was magic, and not the kind I could conjure.

"Okay, so you've gotta tell me," I said, nudging her lightly. "Why Everpine?"

"What do you mean?" she asked, brow furrowing.

"I mean... you're young. Why settle down in a tiny town like this? Where half your customers are old couples, and the other half are... old couples."

She snorted. "Everpine is not full of old people."

"Oh, really? Almost everyone who came into the booth today looked like they were one wrong step away from a hip replacement."

She laughed, the sound bouncing off the trees, settling low in my stomach, and pulling something loose in my chest.

"Okay, fine," she said. "But you said 'almost,' which means not everyone."

"Fair." I shrugged.

Her smile faded a little as her gaze turned forward again. "I was working in Boston. Living for my career. I wanted to be a Michelin chef." She said it softly now, the words turning delicate. "I had this amazing mentor, Maggie. She taught me everything I know. Not just about baking, but about... life."

I didn't interrupt. I didn't joke. I just let her keep talking. Her voice didn't shake yet, but I could feel it might.

"So why did you leave?" I asked gently.

She chewed on her bottom lip. "There was a fire. A stove malfunctioned. I'd put soup on the stove and stepped out, to cry, actually." She exhaled a shaky breath. "My boyfriend had broken up with me. Over text."

I winced. "Classy."

"Right?" She gave a hollow laugh. "Anyway, I asked Maggie to watch the soup while I got myself together. Then..." Her voice caught. "Then the malfunction happened. The stove exploded. A lot of people were hurt. And Maggie..." Her eyes went distant. "Maggie died."

I stopped walking, just barely, and turned to look at her. She didn't look at me. She was too busy staring at the snow like it might hold her together.

"Stella, I'm sorry," I whispered. My hand hovered at her back for a second. Then I did something I never do, I let it land gently, just between her shoulder blades.

She didn't pull away.

She wiped at the corners of her eyes with her sleeve. "After that, I didn't want the big city, that fast life. I just wanted quiet. Simple. I actually typed into the search engine: 'What are the smallest towns in the U.S.'" She gave a soft, embarrassed laugh.

And I laughed too, but it was quieter than usual. Because everything about this woman suddenly made more sense. The fire in her. The walls. The weight in her smile. She'd lost something. She'd built something. And she was still standing.

"This is why I'm so freaked out about the shop. It's my way to honor Maggie. Sugar & Snow is her legacy through me." She blinked up at me, a small smile tugging at her lips. "Guess that explains the grumpy baker act, huh?"

"No," I said, and she blinked.

"What?"

"I think you were always a little grumpy."

A beat passed.

She huffed a laugh. "Asshole."

But she didn't pull away when my hand brushed hers again.

And for the next block, we walked in silence, her fingers brushing mine every few steps, pretending like it was an accident. I just kept looking forward, hoping that I could hide my grin with each touch.

"Okay, first stop." I pointed to the ice skating rink.

She stopped dead. "Absolutely not."

I tilted my head and groaned dramatically. "Why not? Because it's fun?"

Her eyes narrowed. "I can be fun."

"Oh yeah," I said, already striding toward the skate rentals. "That's exactly what fun people say."

Ten minutes later, we were on the ice, well, I was on the ice. Stella was clinging to the rails like her life depended on it.

"I hate you so much," she muttered.

"Because I'm fun?" I teased, skating backwards in front of her like a show-off.

She pushed off, shaky but determined, and made it a full three seconds before she yelped and pitched forward.

I caught her, one arm around her waist, one hand on her wrist, and her body collided against mine. The world around us froze as electricity crackled through my veins when our skin touched. She looked up, lips parted, cheeks flushed from the cold. Her fingers curled against my chest. Her breath hitched.

And God, she was beautiful, not just in the I-want-to-strip-you kind of way, but in the way that made me want to wrap her in a blanket and never let her carry weight alone again.

"Careful," I murmured. "Wouldn't want you to fall for me."

She snorted, shoving me away, but a small smile tugged at the corner of her lips.

We skated a little longer, her clinging to my arm now instead of the rails. I didn't make a big deal of it, even though her fingers curled tighter every time she slipped and caught herself on me. Her laughter came easier now. Softer, more real.

At one point, she stumbled again, and this time, when I caught her, she didn't pull away right away. Her hand lingered on my chest. Her eyes flicked up at me, and amusement danced behind them.

"I'm still not having fun," she lied.

I leaned closer. "Your smile says otherwise."

She flushed and turned away, muttering something under her breath about me being insufferable.

After a while, when her ankles started to ache and her cheeks were pinker than usual, I took mercy on her, and we returned the skates.

Chapter 8
Nick
December 22.

After skating, we wandered into the Christmas Market, which was somehow more festive than the North Pole. The stalls glowed with golden lights, garlands wound around every wooden post, and carolers sang softly near the square. The scent of roasted chestnuts, cinnamon, and woodsmoke wrapped around us like a warm blanket.

Stella walked ahead slightly, stopping to browse at a stand filled with handmade ornaments. She reached for a delicate glass snowflake and held it up to the light.

"It's beautiful," she murmured, more to herself than me.

"You are," I said automatically, even surprising myself.

She rolled her eyes while carefully placing the snowflake back. "Don't you have an off button?"

I chuckled. "You need to find it, Sweetheart."

She muttered something under her breath that definitely wasn't merry, and moved toward the next booth, one selling mulled wine and candied apples. She handed me a steaming cup of wine while keeping an apple and the wine for herself.

"Hey, no apple for me?" I pouted, which seemed to spark her up.

"Hey, no roof for me?" She shot back.

Touché

I took a long sip from the wine, trying to hide my smirk, and immediately regretted it. My mouth lit up like Rudolph's nose.

"Shhhhit. Buhhhhned," I groaned, tongue sticking out like a wounded soldier, fanning my mouth dramatically.

Stella blinked at me, unimpressed. "For God's sake, how are you still alive? How are you, *Santa*?"

But the corners of her mouth twitched like she was seconds away from cracking.

"Yhour so mheaan," I said my tongue still sticking out.

Stella sipped her wine with zero sympathy. "You crashed into my shop. I'm allowed to be mean."

"Okay, what can I do to get you to forgive me?" I pulled my tongue back in, trying to sound innocent.

She raised an eyebrow. "Can you turn back time?"

I chuckle. "And deprive you of my company?"

That did it. She slammed her wine down on the market table and narrowed her eyes. "Oh, because you think you're such an amazing company? Let's recap what's happened to me in the *two and a half days* you've been here, shall we?"

Now *I was* getting annoyed. "Okay, real talk, what's your problem?"

She sighed dramatically. "Do you want a list now, or can I post it later to the North Pole?"

"Hilarious," I muttered, sipping my wine. "Truly, and here I thought we were bonding."

"Well, it's hard to bond when you keep hitting on me like it's your full-time job and act like the whole world is just a joke!"

I hesitated. Maybe she wasn't wrong. But the truth was, when I flirted with her, it wasn't a joke. It was the only way I knew how to say I cared, without saying it.

"Well, if you *hate* me flirting with you so much... why wear something that makes it so damn hard to behave?" I pointed to her outfit, instantly regretting it, but not enough to stop.

Excuse me?" she let out a sharp, high laugh. "I dress up for *me*."

"Mm-hmm. Keep telling yourself that, Sweetheart."

Her mouth parted, eyes wide with disbelief. "Oh, please, Santa. You couldn't handle me. You're all bark, the kind of dog that growls until someone scratches behind his ears, then rolls over like a lapdog."

That's it. Something in me snapped. But not with anger, with something *hotter*. And maybe, if I were being honest, a little desperate to prove her wrong. I stepped in close, closing the gap between us. Her breath hitched; each rise and fall of her chest was mesmerizing.

"Oh, really?" I said, my voice dark and low. "Wanna bet?"

She held my gaze, chin up, and pulse fluttering at her throat. Then she smirked. "Sure, if you want to lose."

I couldn't even think. My fingers wrapped around her wrist firmly, and I guided her towards the prop gingerbread house, which had just cleared out. She squeaked at the sudden movement, but didn't resist. That tiny sound sent a rush straight to my cock. And somewhere, in the far back of my mind, I knew I was teetering on something more than lust.

The second we stepped inside, and the door slammed shut behind us, I conjured a glowing lock with a flick of my fingers. It clicked softly, making sure no one would bother us.

Inside, the air was warm, thick with sugar and spice filtering in from the market. I pinned her firmly against the candy-brick wall. Her breath stuttered, chest rising fast, and I pressed in close enough for her to feel exactly what she was doing to me.

"So you think I can't handle you?" I murmured, mouth trailing down the side of her neck, then lower, right across her collarbone.

She worked down a swallow before answering. "Please, you're Santa. Santa is not naughty." Every word spilled from her lips like a challenge.

My gaze dropped. She wasn't wearing a bra. Her nipples were tight under the fabric of her dress, practically begging. I slid my hand up her sides, slow and teasing, until I reached her chest. I cupped her, dragged my thumb across one perfect peak. She shuddered from my touch.

"Oh, Sweetheart..." I dragged my thumb in a lazy circle over her nipple, felt it pebble even tighter through the fabric. "You have *no* idea how naughty Santa can be."

Her lips parted. A sound caught in her throat, like she wanted to argue, but couldn't remember how words worked.

I leaned in and let my voice drop low and filthy. "Let me show you."

Before she could've shot back a snarky comment, I summoned it. In my palm, a candy cane appeared. Thick and slick with glossy red and white swirl that pulsed faintly with magic, vibrating low like a hum of anticipation. I'm no stranger to using magic to create such items, but this one was special just for her. A little holiday spirit, if you will.

Her eyes widened. "Is that a...?"

"A candy cane," I confirmed, voice low. "With a few... upgrades."

I pressed the button at the base. It buzzed to life with a sinful sound, a low, hungry purr that filled the space between us.

Under my other hand, I felt her heartbeat spike. She shifted, thighs clenching together instinctively.

I leaned in, lips brushing the shell of her ear. "Sensitive, Sweetheart?"

I trailed the candy cane down her body, slow and deliberate, letting it buzz against her ribs, her stomach, and just above the hem of her dress. The air between us pulsed, thick with heat and magic. But it wasn't just that. We both knew we were about to cross a line.

"Last chance to back out, Sweetheart."

Say no. Say stop. Please. Because if you don't, I don't know how I'll be able to let you go.

"What? Too afraid you will lose?" She taunted, and a wicked grin etched on my face.

I reached down, fingers skimming over her tights, and with a swift, decisive tug, I tore a hole clean through them. A gasp fell from her lips as I trailed my index finger over her thong. Black lace and already soaked through. My cock twitched from the touch of it.

I let my thumb graze the damp fabric, slow and filthy, until her breath hitched and her hips shifted toward me.

I reached between us, dragging the candy cane vibrator slowly across her soaked lace, letting it thrum against the fabric. Her legs jolted

"Ohh, fuuuck."

Her sweet moan vibrated through my body. Her back arched, and her hips rolled against the cane, desperate for more friction. I shifted the toy and pressed harder against her clit.

I watched her squirm, hips twitching with every buzz of the toy. She was soaked, lace clinging to her, trembling with need.

"Look at you," I murmured, voice thick, heavy. "Just from this?"

She didn't answer, couldn't. Her mouth was slack, eyes glazed, breath coming in quick little gasps. I hooked a finger under her thong, dragging the drenched fabric to the side.

"Still think Santa's not naughty?"

Her only answer was a breathless moan as the cold air hit her bare, soaked pussy. I let the tip of the candy cane brush against her heat. She shuddered in response, and her cheeks were already tinted in a beautiful pink blush.

Slowly, I aligned the thick end of it to her entrance and coated it with her arousal. Her knees buckled from the sensation. I caught her with one hand on her thigh, spreading it wider.

I clicked the button again, increasing the intensity, and a whimper escaped from her.

"P-please..." Her lips trembled; that slight movement almost made me lose control.

"You want this?" I asked while sliding the tip into her, causing her to cry out.

"Shhh, Sweetheart." I taunted, "You don't want the whole market to hear how naughty you are."

She bit her lips, trying to muffle her moans.

"Good girl," I growled. I couldn't even hide the want in my voice. "Do you want more, baby?"

She nodded frantically, her chest heaving.

"Use your words, Sweetheart. You have such a big mouth on you. Use it." I grinned, holding the cane in place, watching her hips buckle, desperate for more.

"I want it, please." She whimpered, her thighs trembled under my hands.

"That's it," I added another inch, her fingers scrabbled at the fragile wall behind her, trying to ground herself.

"You're soaked, baby. Practically dripping all over this toy." I murmured and couldn't decide whether to watch her face or her glistening pussy.

Another inch and I shifted the angle, grinding it against that sweet spot inside her, pinning her back to the wall.

"I would say, I can handle you just fine," I said, and her eyes fluttered shut, but I couldn't let that. I wanted her to see me, to see us. "Open them, baby."

Her defiance was still in her, forcing her eyes closed, so I twisted the toy, shoving it deeper, and her eyes popped open. My other hand found her nipple again, rolling the peak over the shirt.

With one final thrust, I bottomed out the toy, angling the curved end to her clit. Her head fell back, and her hips moved in waves. Pretty lips parted as silent cries fell from them.

I leaned in, brushing her lips without kissing. Her breath stuttered again. Something *melted* in the space between us.

I began to move the cane in and out in a steady rhythm, watching as her face twisted in pleasure.

"Harder." She sobbed, bucking her hips against the toy.

Who am I to deny her what she wants?

I clicked to the next setting and started to fuck her harder; her breath became shallow, and as her hands settled on my shoulder, I could feel her whole body shaking.

Her sweet pussy clenched around the toy firmer and firmer. Each thrust made her dig her nail into me.

"Fuck." She breathed, her eyes rolled to the back of her head, and her whole body tensed up.

"You going to come, Sweetheart?" I asked fucking her harder.

She tried to nod, but I could see she was standing at the edge. I pressed the button again, setting it to the maximum.

A scream left her lips as her body bowed and legs shook. She clamped around the toy, coming hard, soaking it with her sweet juices. She was riding, chasing the high, and I couldn't help but mutter dirty praises for my good girl.

I dropped to my knees watching as her cunt strangles the toy, and I couldn't help myself, her pussy looked so goddam good my mouth watered. While she still rode her orgasm, I glued my mouth to her, sucking on her clit.

She grasped my hair, both trying to push it away and pulling it closer. I feasted on her cunt like a man who hasn't eaten in years, and it felt like it would never be enough. Her arousal glided down my throat, and it was sweeter than any nectar I could ever taste.

Her body tensed up again, her fingers dug into my scalp, as I worked the vibrator in her, sucking her clit. My hand slid to her ass, pulling her closer to me if that was even possible.

"Oh God...Fuck...fuck" Stella was out of her mind. She closed her arms around my head and came all over my face.

Her body sagged, and she clung to me, her chest heaving. I showered her with kisses all over her pussy, her inner thigh, as I pulled the vibrator out of her.

I rose to my feet, tucking a damp strand of her hair behind her ears.

"I think you're officially on the top of the naughty list," I murmured.

She laughed, still foggy. We stayed like that for a moment, our breaths syncing, and the heat between us growing. My forehead leaned against hers while she toyed with my sweater. She looked up at me, her lips parted and eyes simmering.

I leaned in just enough for both of our breaths to hitch, just enough that our lips almost brushed together.

And God help me, I wanted to kiss her for real.

Jingle.

We both froze.

"I might be still hazy from the orgasm, was that...?

I straightened, my head jolting towards the door.

Jingle-Jingle-Jingle.

Outside, murmurs were growing louder, footsteps becoming rapid.

"Oh my God, is that a reindeer?" Someone yelped outside.

Stella swore, scrambling to fix her dress, wiping at her mouth, cheeks still flushed.

I evaporated the candy cane, and we burst out of the gingerbread house together, scanning the area.

I don't know which one of my reindeer was in the area, but they were serious cockblockers.

Chapter 9
Stella
December 22.

Snow crunched under our boots as we tore through the market. People gasped and squeaked at the unexpected guest barreling past their booths.

I was still breathless, my legs jelly, my thighs aching, and my entire body buzzing from the frankly unholy orgasm that Santa-freaking-Claus had just given me.

A blur of antlers darted past a spice stand.

"There!" Nick shouted, pointing. "DANCER!"

Everyone looked at us, confused and wide-eyed.

This idiot didn't get the memo that Santa is just a myth?

Heads whipped around. Someone dropped their cup of cocoa. A kid gasped. A tourist started filming.

Oh. My. God.

I forced a tight laugh and waved him off like he was just some unhinged holiday LARPer.

"Yeah...Dancer! Totally. You think Rudolph's showing up later, too?" I asked, eyes wide, grin tight.

A ripple of laughter spread through the crowd. Someone joked that Dasher was doing shots behind the gingerbread booth. My shoulders sagged in relief.

Nick shot me a glare, muttering under his breath, "I really hope Rudolf will show up."

I snorted. "You're lucky you're hot."

Dancer spotted Nick and, in a matter of seconds, he took off, barreling through the market.

And just like that... *Reindeer parkour number two.*

Fuck.

Dancer dashed through the booths, knocking over ornaments and decorations. Nick swore and bolted after him. I gave it half a second before I groaned, hitched up my ruined tights, and followed.

"This is not how I imagined the night would end!" I huffed, my ribs aching from the sprint.

"Don't tell me a little reindeer chasing is not a good afterplay." Nick tilted his head, shouting back.

He enjoyed this a little too much.

We tore through the Christmas market, past stunned vendors and horrified carolers. Dancer hurdled a candy cane archway like he'd been training for this his whole life. And at the sight of the candy cane, warmth spread across my cheeks, which had nothing to do with running a half-marathon.

"Why are the reindeer so fast?" I yelled, barely dodging a family taking a photo with a twelve-foot inflatable snowman. It was more of a rhetorical question, but that didn't stop Nick from answering it.

"We need to fly over the whole world in one night somehow."

Dancer rounded the corner near the hot cocoa fountain, yes, fountain, and launched himself onto a table stacked with fruitcake samples. The entire thing collapsed under him.

A marshmallow shot through the air and smacked a child in the forehead. Someone screamed. Someone else cheered.

Nick skidded past the chaos, slipping slightly on a spilled custard tart. "He's heading for the carousel!"

"Of course he is," I muttered, dodging a rogue fruitcake chunk.

He zipped past a popcorn stand, narrowly avoiding a toddler with a balloon animal, and made a sharp turn, straight for the carousel.

Dancer leapt onto the moving platform like he was making a stage entrance. His hooves clattered against the painted wood, and he somehow managed to *pirouette* mid-gallop.

Nick skidded to a stop beside me. "He's... dancing."

I couldn't help but giggle. "Well, he *is* Dancer after all."

The reindeer was now prancing between plastic unicorns and swan-shaped benches, antlers twinkling with stolen tinsel, his tail flicking like he was performing to an invisible panel of holiday judges. The carousel spun, lights flashing, music blaring, children screaming in a mix of terror and delight.

"Oh my god," I whispered. "He's waiting for us to chase him."

Nick groaned. "I hate how theatrical he is."

I blinked. "I cannot believe this is my life."

And then, just as we started creeping toward the edge of the carousel, Dancer, dramatic bastard that he is, vaulted.

Not off the side. No. He *leapt* over the golden reindeer statue at the center, did a show-off spin midair, and landed with a thud on the *roof* of the carousel.

Gasps rippled through the market. Someone screamed. The music kept playing. Nick cursed under his breath.

"He's up there now?!"

Dancer struck a pose.

Literally.

Chest out. Antlers proud. Legs positioned like he was about to accept a bouquet and bow.

A flick of his wrist, and a rope of enchanted ribbon shimmered to life in the air, curling like a lasso. "We're ending this. Right now."

He tossed the rope skyward. It arced cleanly over Dancer, who *waited*, and as soon as it caught around his middle, the reindeer huffed like an offended celebrity caught in a scandal.

Nick yanked. Dancer *slid dramatically* down the side of the carousel roof, landed in a pile of fake snow, and lay there.

I jogged over, out of breath and out of patience, and snapped the glowing cuffs around his front legs before he could stage a comeback tour.

"You know," I said, panting, "It's kinda cute. He just wanted to perform."

Nick muttered a string of curses under his breath, something about how he could "perform to the elves for all he cared", but his eyes were smiling.

"Three down," he said, catching his breath.

Around us, people had stopped walking. Some stared. Others gawked openly. A kid pointed. A woman filmed.

"Nick." I hissed, but he was too busy lecturing Dancer.

"... and the next time you want to perform," he scolded, "you'll ask first. We'll get lights, a proper venue..."

"NICK!" Okay, this wasn't a hiss anymore, but he snapped his head towards me, towards the crowd.

A beat passed, and I could practically see the gears turning in his head.

Then, without missing a beat: "Ta-da!"

He threw his arms wide and bowed as he'd just finished a Broadway show. Then, unbelievably, nudged Dancer to do the same. The reindeer lifted his head slightly and gave a reluctant little nod.

Nick looked over at me, still smiling like a maniac. "Bow, Sweetheart."

I blinked at him. "What?"

"Go on."

With a groan, I rolled my eyes and gave a quick, stiff bow.

Nick turned back to the crowd. "Hope you enjoyed our little holiday show, 'Chasing the Lost Reindeer.' Just a bit of holiday magic and, uh, cutting-edge tech. Nothing to worry about, folks!"

People chuckled. A few clapped. One guy even asked if Dancer was available for birthday parties. Nick waved as he'd just been crowned Mr. Christmas, and once the crowd finally dispersed, we collapsed onto the nearest bench, hearts pounding, cheeks burning.

Snow started falling again. Soft, slow, like powdered sugar.

Nick bumped my shoulder with his. "So... wanna make out, or...?"

He said it like a joke, but not in his usual 'I make a joke out of everything' way. Just to break the tension that was simmering beneath the surface. But his words made my stomach twist. Everything that just happened between us started to feel too real.

A walking myth who wasn't supposed to make me feel this unsteady. This *real*. Who would leave as soon as this insane holiday mess was over, back to the North Pole?

I pushed off the bench, trying to avoid his gaze, and his smile faltered.

"Let's just go home, please," I said, not looking at him.

Nick didn't argue. He just nodded once and stood beside me.

We walked back in silence. As soon as we got home, I bolted for my room, slammed the door, and locked it behind me. Then I slid down the wall, buried my face in my hands, and spent the rest of the night cursing myself.

This shouldn't happen. I knew if this were just a fling, I would be fine. I had my fair share of one-night stands, but this...with him, it was different.

Something sparked in my chest every time he looked at me, and it wasn't just annoyance or arousal or adrenaline from chasing reindeer through the streets. It was something quieter. Scarier. Something that curled beneath my ribs and made me feel like maybe, just maybe... I wanted more.

And I didn't want to admit it. Not to him. Not to myself.

Because he was leaving, because *of course* he was.

Because Christmas Eve was almost here, and I knew what that meant. He'd get the sleigh, he'd save the holiday, and he'd go.

And all of this?

The heat between us in the gingerbread house. The way our fingers brushed when we walked through town, and neither of us pulled away. The way he always caught me when I slipped on the ice, like he was ready for it before I was. His stupid jokes and flirting.

It will all be just a ridiculous faded memory. But the worst part was that I didn't want this to be just a memory.

I didn't want to forget the way he looked at me. I didn't want to forget how it felt when he touched me like he knew what I needed before I said it. I didn't want to forget the way my whole body lit up around him, not just with lust, but with something deeper. Something terrifying.

How would I feel if I actually slept with him? Would I be stupid enough to hope he might stay?

No. No, I couldn't let that happen.

Especially not when I had no idea what this was for him. Maybe he was just looking for a warm body, a quick fling, something to pass the time until his magic kicked back in and he could fly away.

I pressed my palms over my face, trying to steady my breathing.

I could hear him pacing downstairs, but I forced myself to ignore him.

I dropped onto my bed and pulled the pillow over my head, and somehow sleep had mercy on me, and I drifted off into a dreamless slumber.

Chapter 10

Nick
December 23

Stella walked into the kitchen, hair a mess, shoulders tight. She looked like she hadn't slept. Not that I'd fared much better. Between the reindeer stampede and, you know, me giving her a screaming orgasm against a gingerbread wall, neither of us had exactly gotten our full eight hours. I could see she was struggling, and I felt awful that I was too rough with her yesterday.

She froze when she saw me already at the counter, holding two mugs, hot cocoa with coffee, and an ungodly amount of marshmallows.

"Morning," I offered gently.

"Is it?" she said, eyeing me as if I might explode.

I held out the mug. "Peace offering."

She took it, fingers brushing mine. "That's not necessary, Nick. But thanks."

I stepped closer, slowly. Careful. Her walls were up, but I needed her to hear me.

"Hey," I said. "I just wanted to say I'm sorry if I pushed you into something you didn't want. If I misread you yesterday. If I were too rough."

She blinked, like she hadn't expected that. Her eyes shimmered. "No. It's not that." She laughed sharply in surprise. "Trust me. It's just... you're going to leave."

My chest tightened. Because yeah. That was always the ending. And that was what kept me up all night as well. I kept thinking how I could manage to stay here, to stay with her, because in only three days she turned my world upside down, and I knew the reason for it.

Soulmates.

The word echoed through my chest like a bell, low and constant. I tried to push it down, tried to reason it away. But I'd heard stories. I *knew* the signs: that instant pull, that impossible magnetism. The way time bends around someone like them, finally making the world make sense.

Like finding quiet in a loud room. Like drifting on an ocean and suddenly hitting shore.

And *she* was that for me, even if I didn't want to admit it, even if it scared the hell out of me.

She continued, voice soft. "And no matter how much I might want to take things further, I can't. Because I don't feel like I can promise myself that my heart will be safe."

God, that hurt.

Not because she was wrong. Because she was so damn right.

She shouldn't feel safe with me. I didn't even know what would happen after Christmas Eve. I didn't know if I could bend the rules, or break them, or find a loophole that would let me stay in this small town with the only person who's ever made me forget the weight of centuries.

I wanted to tell her. Everything. About how I wasn't sure I could leave either. About how I could feel it in my chest, this wasn't casual. This wasn't temporary.

But I didn't. I stayed quiet for a while. Just stood there, mug in hand, heart heavy. Her words echoed what I'd been trying to ignore since the first time she yelled at me.

This thing between us wasn't supposed to happen. Not in three days. Not like this. But she'd looked at me like I wasn't just some immortal idiot with a magic sleigh. She saw me.

"Yes," I finally said. "You're right."

Her face flickered. Something deflated behind her eyes. And I hated that I was the one who put it there.

I cleared my throat. "But I have a plan."

She arched her brow. "Should I be afraid?"

I sipped my cocoa, smirking over the rim. "If we find Rudolph... the rest will follow."

She blinked. "You're serious?"

"Dead serious. He's their leader. The others are magical, sure, but Rudolph has the pull. If he comes back willingly, they all do."

"And you're just telling me this now?"

"You were busy locking yourself in your room."

She glared. I smiled. It felt good to slide back into this rhythm. Her fuming. Me provoking. Like armor we both wore so that the truth wouldn't cut too deep.

"So we find Rudolph," she said. "How?"

I pulled out the old tracking map. A glowing red dot pulsed near the edge.

"Old school spell. Still had some juice left." I tapped the dot. "He's close. Somewhere in town. If we head out before nightfall, we might beat the holiday rush."

She leaned in. Her hair brushed my arm. I didn't move.

"You think he's just... what? Hanging out at the mall?" she asked. "Getting his hooves buffed?"

"Could be, he's the most dramatic of them all."

She laughed. And damn it, it hit me straight in the gut. That sound. That smile. I wanted to bottle it. Keep it.

"Okay," she said. "We find Rudolph. The others come back. You save Christmas."

My smile faltered. "And I go home."

There it was. The inevitable goodbye.

She looked down. "Right."

I nudged her mug with mine. "Hey."

She glanced up.

I gave her the smallest smile I could manage without falling apart. "Let's find him first. The rest... We'll figure it out."

And for a second, she looked like she believed me.

After breakfast, we set up the booth, well, *Stella* set up the booth. I hovered nearby, doing what could generously be called "supervising," but really just involved moving a spoon from one side of the counter to the other.

But hey, last time I tried baking and helping with the cookies was a complete disaster. So technically, I was helping by not helping.

She was already in overdrive, falling into that laser-focused rhythm she had when she worked, eyebrows scrunched, lips pursed, flour on her cheek. Dangerous combination. I had to force myself not to watch her too closely, not to let my mind drift to what her hands had been doing last night, or what I wanted them to do again.

"Is everything ready outside?" She asked as she rolled out some dough.

"Yes, Boss." I nodded. "Should I help or...?"

"Please don't." She laughed, but then nudged her head towards the sink. "You can do the dishes."

"Wow," I deadpanned. "Truly living the Santa dream."

I rolled up my sleeves and got to work, scrubbing plates while she attacked a new tray of dough with focused violence. For a few minutes, we fell into something that almost felt domestic, comfortable. Quiet. The only sounds were the splash of water and the steady rhythm of her rolling pin.

Then she huffed and tried to blow a strand of hair out of her face with a sharp puff of air. Adorable.

"Okay," she said, pausing with her hands on her hips. "You've got to tell me. What's the North Pole really like? I can't believe I haven't asked that yet."

I chuckled, rinsing a mug. "Honestly? I'm impressed you lasted this long. Most people ask the second they hear the word 'Santa.' Usually followed by, 'Is it cold?' and, 'Where are the reindeer?'"

"Well, I've *seen* the reindeer," she muttered. "Up close. In action. I'm good."

She reached for a cookie sheet, then paused, brows furrowing.

"Wait...hold up. Do a *lot* of people know about Santa?"

I chuckled, shaking my head.

"Oh, God no. Most people don't want to believe. It's easier not to. But there are a *few*, kids, mostly. Those who need something a little extra. A little more hope. Magic. I visit them sometimes. Not for presents, just... to remind them the world can still surprise you."

Her expression softened.

"They remember?" she asked quietly.

"They do," I said. "But they're young. Give it a few years, and most will convince themselves it was a dream. Something they imagined. A fluke."

Her mouth shaped an 'o', and she returned to her dough.

I turned to lean against the counter, drying my hands on a dish towel. "It's... magical. I mean the North Pole. Like, actually magical. Big central village with old-style cobbled streets, gingerbread trim on everything, twinkling lights that never burn out. We've got snow that sparkles on its own, chimneys that clean themselves.

She laughed under her breath, but her eyes were soft. Curious.

"The main center is huge. Like, you could walk across it for days if you weren't magical. There's a massive toy development wing, a bakery, though nowhere near *this* good, an engineering hub, stables, sleigh garage..."

"Of course, there's a sleigh garage," she said, shaking her head.

"Elves run the show," I went on. "And no, they're not what you think. No bells on their shoes. No cartoon nonsense. Just regular folks with pointy ears and too much energy. Most of them do wear green and red, but that's by *choice*, okay?" I held up my hands as if I were being interrogated.

Stella snorted. "Right. Big elf fashion movement going on up there."

"Hey, they like consistency," I said, grinning. "But otherwise? It's just a functioning society. Everyone has a home. A job. A family. They celebrate birthdays, have schools, date, sometimes messily. Elves live about twice as long as humans, which means their teenage years are a nightmare."

She blinked. "Wait. Don't tell me they have drama."

"Oh, you have *no idea*," I said with a dramatic sigh. "The North Pole has more drama than a Hallmark movie marathon."

Stella leaned against the opposite counter, her arms crossed, smiling, and something warm bloomed behind my ribs.

I wanted this. I wanted *her*. And I had no idea how the hell I was going to leave.

I kept talking, filling the space with stories from the North Pole, half to distract her, and half to convince myself that this wasn't as bad as it felt. She laughed at my jokes, tried to hide it behind her hand like I wouldn't notice. But I did. Every smile. Every eye-roll. Every time her cheeks went pink from something I said that probably should've stayed in my head.

Then the shop opened, and the rest of the day blurred into something that looked a hell of a lot like domestic bliss. Stella kneaded dough as her life depended on it. I poured cocoa for sugar-high kids and grumpy parents. She called out orders. I wiped down the counters. She muttered curses when the cookies spread too wide. I told her they still looked perfect.

We worked side by side, moved around each other like we'd been doing this forever.

Holy Shit.

Am I falling in love? Oh God. This is not good. How do I stop this?

Do I want to stop it?

After we packed up, we gathered around the map again, and I tapped it frantically. The pulsing red dot shimmered, then blinked twice.

"That's new," I muttered.

Stella frowned. "What does that mean?"

"It means the spell's unstable. Someone's interfering. Or he's on the move."

"Can they trick the spell?"

I wanted to lie. But I didn't. "They're chaos incarnate. I'm lucky this thing works at all."

"Great," she muttered. "So we're chasing a magic glitch through town based on a glowing dot with commitment issues."

"Sounds like a date to me."

She gave me a look. I grinned, already grabbing my coat.

We followed the blinking dot through Everpine, weaving past ice sculptures and fudge stands. A few people waved. One older woman asked if I was the hot guy from the lumberjack calendar.

I winked. Stella made a noise like she wanted to strangle me with tinsel. Suddenly, the dot on the map flared bright and pinged like a microwave.

"Here!" I spun around. "He's close."

We turned the corner. Fresh hoof prints marked the snow near the Christmas trees.

I crouched, touched one. "Still warm."

A blur of brown and antlers darted past the end of the street.

"Rudolph?" Stella shouted.

I squinted. "No glow. Not Rudolph."

The blur paused, huffed, and then sneezed explosively.

"Blitzen," I said. "He's allergic to tinsel."

He let out a proud snort and trotted toward a cocoa stand. Head-butted the marshmallow jar.

"Oh for the love of..."

I bolted after him. I've done more cardio in the last few days than in a millennium. Stella followed me, dodging mistletoe couples and elf-ear vendors. We cornered him by the Ferris wheel. He was licking frosting off a dropped cookie.

I muttered a quick spell. A glowing harness shimmered over him, locking into place. He huffed once, then stood still like a scolded toddler.

"One more down," I said, breathing hard. "We need to find Rudolph."

"And he's still moving?"

I looked at the map. The dot had shifted again. Closer to the town square.

"Yep," I said. "And if we don't catch him soon... Christmas might really go to hell."

Chapter 11
Stella
December 23

The town square was mainly quiet now, just a few stragglers finishing their cocoa or their mulled wine, laughing in little groups under the string lights.

Holiday music played from somewhere overhead.

Everything felt... like Christmas.

Everpine always leaned hard into December, tourists arrived in flocks as they gawked at the white lights scalloping from lamppost to lamppost, while they declared our main street was "quaint," But somehow this Christmas, the season felt heightened. I could've stayed locked in this snow globe of a town forever... given that Nick was by my side.

His coat brushed mine with every step. We hadn't said much since we caught Blitzen. I wasn't sure if it was the adrenaline, the magic... or the terrifying ache in my chest I'd been trying to ignore every time I looked at him. We walked back to the house and dropped off Blitzen, then strolled the town hoping to catch Rudolf.

My limbs went numb from the cold, and I was just about to suggest that we head back home when he suddenly stopped.

I glanced up to see why, and there it was. Hanging from a crooked wooden arch between two booths: a sprig of mistletoe tied with red ribbon.

Seriously?

Nick followed my gaze. He stared at it, then at me. A playful glow sparkled behind his eyes.

"Nope." I turned immediately. "Absolutely not. That's the oldest trick in the..."

But he moved fast. One hand slid around my waist, the other brushed my jaw, tilting my face toward his.

"It's tradition," he said, too casually.

"Nick..." I wanted to kiss him, but every worry I had was still there.

"Kiss me, Stella. Please." His eyes silently begged me. "I know I'll leave. I know this might make things harder. But please, I can't leave without tasting your lips once."

We paused there, frozen in place, breath puffing in the cold air. My gaze dropped to his lips. I rose onto my toes, fingers curling into his coat, and kissed him, soft at first, holding my breath.

He responded instantly, mouth warm, hungry, one hand gripping my hip, the other cradling the back of my neck. When he deepened it, I let him. He pulled my body close to him, and I was melting under his touch. I didn't want to stop. And when I finally pulled back, breathless, he leaned in again.

"We should go home," I whispered, between kisses.

"You sure?" he asked, but he was barely able to stop kissing me. "What about what we talked about?"

"Take me home now, Santa." I breathed.

A wicked grin stretched on his face, and he hauled me up, tossing me over his shoulder.

"Wai...You're gonna carry me all the way home?!"

He just laughed and carried me all the way home, while I shrieked and cursed, but I held on tight, enjoying the way his hands felt around me.

The second we stepped through the door, he started to tear my clothes from my body. Almost quite literally. Everything was frantic, and moments later, I stood there in front of him with just my bra and thong on.

He pulled me toward the couch by the fire, sank into it, legs spread wide, and patted his lap.

"Ever wanted to sit on Santa's lap?" He asked, his voice dripping with desire and mischief.

"Not really." I couldn't help the laugh that bubbled up my throat.

His bright eyes darkened instantly, pupils blowing wide until only a sliver of green remained. "Ever wanted to be bent over Santa's lap and spanked like the naughty little thing you are?"

He barely waited for my slight nod. His hand clamped around my wrist, and he yanked me forward. My feet stumbled over the rug; the room tilted, and suddenly my stomach slammed across his hard thighs, ass angled high in the air, toes barely brushing the floor. The heat of the fire licked my bare skin; the cool leather kissed my breasts where they spilled from the bra. I felt deliciously helpless, pinned by nothing but his grip and the weight of his gaze.

His palm settled on the curve of my ass, possessive, testing. Then his thumb began tracing slow, deliberate circles over the lace of my thong, each rotation dragging the fabric tighter against my clit until it throbbed in time with my pulse. I squirmed, a whimper slipping free.

"You have to tell me if it's too much." Anticipation twisted in my stomach. "If I am being too rough, you say that word, and it stops. Got it, Sweetheart?"

"Yes," I nodded, the motion frantic, my thighs already drenched, slickness coating the inside of them like evidence I couldn't hide.

His palm cracked down on my ass harder than I expected, a white-hot bloom across my right cheek that tore a sharp cry from my throat. My whole body jerked forward over his lap, toes curling against the rug.

"That's my good girl." He pressed a soft kiss to my temple, beard tickling my skin. "So fucking beautiful like this."

The praise pooled low in my belly, warm and liquid. I was starving for more.

Another slap, softer this time, a gentle sting that made my head fall forward, his name slipping out on a broken whimper.

"Are you wet for me, sweetheart?" he murmured, fingers sliding between my legs, tracing the soaked lace like he already knew the answer.

"Y-yes." The word cracked in half as he tugged my thong aside and dipped his index finger into me, slow, deliberate, curling just enough to make my eyes roll back.

"Jesus, listen to that," he whispered, voice reverent, sliding deeper, adding a second finger until I was stretched around him, clenching helplessly. "Hear how greedy your pussy is? Sucking me in like it's been waiting all night for this."

I couldn't answer, just a desperate, keening sound that made him chuckle, low and fond.

Another spank hit the curve of my ass, while his fingers pumped in me.

"That's it," he crooned, kissing the shell of my ear. "Ride my fingers, sweetheart. Show me how much you love being my good little girl."

I did, shameless, hips rolling, chasing the slow burn he built so carefully. Every time I got close, he eased off, keeping me on the edge until I was trembling, tears pricking my lashes.

He curled his fingers deeper, thumb circling my clit with devastating precision, then, without warning, his hand lifted and came down in a sharp, wet slap right across my swollen clit.

"Oh my God, Please..." I was sobbing, words pouring out of me without my mind truly forming them. "Please don't stop, I'm gonna... Please make me come."

With a low groan, another slap ended on my clit, and I came undone with a scream I barely muffled against the sofa cushion, toes curling so hard they cramped, thighs clamping around his wrist as wave after wave of blinding pleasure tore through me. My pussy fluttered wildly around his fingers, gushing over his hand, dripping down his wrist, marking the leather beneath us.

He didn't stop. He kept stroking, kept spanking my oversensitive clit in soft, rhythmic taps that dragged every last tremor out of me until I was limp, shaking, and sobbing into the cushion.

"There we go," he whispered, voice thick with awe and tenderness, gathering me close so my cheek rested against his chest. "There's my good girl. Look at you coming so pretty for me, Sweetheart."

I couldn't speak, could only cling to him, aftershocks rippling through me every time he brushed my clit with the pad of his thumb.

He pressed gentle kisses to my temple, my closed eyelids, and the tears on my cheeks, then he lifted me. My vision was still blurry when I felt him positioning himself at my entrance.

"Nick..." I gasped when the blunt tip of his cock brushed against my entrance.

"Tell me you want this, baby." He kissed along my jawline, drawing circles at my entrance. "I need to hear it again."

"Yes." I breathed and lowered myself on him. Inch by inch, my pussy engulfed him, and we both groaned from the sensation.

"Fuck, Stella," he rasped when I took him to the root, voice shredded. "You feel so good. So fucking perfect around me."

When he finally bottomed out, we just stayed like that for a moment, our breaths syncing and foreheads pressed together.

I started to move, slow, deliberate rolls of my hips, savoring every dragging inch of him. The stretch burned into bliss; the burn blurred into pure, electric pleasure. I could feel every ridge, every pulse, the way he throbbed inside me like he was trying to fuse us together forever.

His hands held me firmly, guiding me, while his mouth crashed into mine, devouring me like he can't get enough of my taste. His tongue swallowed greedily every moan that slipped past my lips.

I sped up, chasing the climb, thighs trembling. Each downward slide slammed him against that spot that turned my vision white at the edges. His grip tightened, bruising in the best way, urging me faster.

With a savage growl, he hooked his fingers into the lace cups of my bra and ripped. Fabric tore like paper; my breasts spilled free, nipples pebbling instantly in the cool air. Nick didn't hesitate; he dipped his head and closed his mouth over one aching peak, sucking hard, and his teeth grazing just enough to make me sob.

The pleasure burned low inside my stomach, my core fluttered with each brutal thrust, and clit swollen and throbbing against his pelvis on every grind.

I ran my fingers through his silver locks, yanking him closer to my chest, arching into his mouth. My pussy clamped down harder around him, and the room was filled with my uncontrolled moans.

"Nick..." I whimpered, feeling my orgasm building stronger and stronger inside me.

"That's it, Sweetheart." He mumbled into my tits. "Come all over my cock, baby."

He continued to suck on my nipples, and the orgasm crashed through me, long and hard. My pussy clenched around him, like it wanted to strangle him. My throat was raw from screaming, but Nick kept thrusting until he coaxed every bit of the orgasm out of me.

He slammed me down one final time, pinning me flush against him, cock buried to the hilt. A guttural growl tore from his chest, deep and animal, and he came with a roar. His cock jerked again and again, emptying everything he had while my pussy milked him greedily for every drop.

We collapsed together, panting our slick bodies glued together. His arms banded around me like steel, crushing me to his chest as the aftershocks rolled through us both.

"Jesus, Sweetheart," he breathed, brushing a few strands of hair back and cupping my face.

A beat passed before I could speak again, my chest tightening.

"You really have to go back?" I whispered.

He pressed a kiss to my cheek, sadness gleaming in his eyes.

"I'm afraid so. Everything I am is tied to that place. I've been away for three days, and I can already feel it pulling me back."

I tried to swallow the lump forming in my throat. "And I can't...?"

"No, Sweetheart." His voice cracked, just slightly. "Humans aren't built for the North Pole. Not for long."

We lay there for a moment, still tangled, still holding on like we could delay time.

"Then we'd better make the most of tonight," I said softly. "Right, Santa?"

He looked up at me, relief and pain flashing behind his gaze. "Oh, sweetheart," he murmured, his voice dark and low. "I just hope you can handle what I plan to do to you."

Chapter 12
Stella
December 24

When I woke up, for one glorious, sleepy second, I thought I'd dreamed the last twenty-four hours. That Santa Claus hadn't made me come at least five times last night, with absolutely no regard for human recovery time. That there weren't magical reindeer scattered across town. That a sleigh crash hadn't wrecked my roof. But then I rolled over, and I could feel all my muscles ache in the best way possible, and there he was.

Nick.

I really did have sex with Santa Claus. Not just any sex. Hot, dirty, and mind-blowing sex.

He lay bare-chested, softly snoring next to me. My heart ached at the sight, knowing this was the last time I would see it. I pressed a careful kiss on his cheek and slipped out of bed.

Barefoot and still naked, I padded into the kitchen and pulled on the closest apron I could find. I started making scrambled eggs and bacon, or at least I tried, when I felt his body press up behind mine.

"Morning, Sweetheart." He murmured, lips brushing my shoulder, and I melted into his touch.

"Morning, Santa," I whispered, eyes fluttering shut as he wrapped his arms around my waist and pulled me flush against him.

"Just the apron?" he groaned in my ear. "You're trying to kill me."

Heat flushed through me. "I wanted to make breakfast quickly. No time to get dressed."

"Mmm-hmm." His hand slid down my back, firm and deliberate. "Lean forward, baby. Let me have my breakfast."

My body bent over the counter, and a second later, he was behind me, dropping to his knees, feasting on me while the eggs hissed and turned to charcoal behind us.

Eventually, on the third attempt, we managed to cook something without setting it on fire.

Nick frowned mid-bite. "Shouldn't we be prepping the booth? People'll be out doing last-minute cookie runs."

I shook my head. "Nope. I decided not to open today."

He blinked. "Really? On Christmas Eve?"

"I want to spend this day with you," I said quietly, then added, "Besides, we still have one stubborn reindeer to catch."

"You sure? Closing on Christmas Eve..." he asked softly.

"I'm sure," I replied instantly, and I meant it. I wasn't going to waste a single minute of our last day together.

"Look, I'm not one for great revelations, but these last few days made me realize that everything I am has been poured into this shop. Because of Maggie... Because of what happened. But I also realized that I can't keep throwing myself into work and letting life pass me by. It's the 24th, Nick. We both know that one way or another, today you'll go back. And since there's no rhyme or reason for us to try some ridiculous long-distance relationship, this means today is our last day together."

Nick watched me for a long moment, expression softening like he wasn't used to someone choosing him back.

"Okay," he murmured, brushing a thumb along my jaw. "Then today is ours."

For a moment, it almost felt normal. Domestic. Warm. Dangerous, in the way that falling for him was starting to feel less like a mistake and more like gravity.

My phone buzzed next to me, playing 'Jingle Bells' as its ringtone. My brows furrowed. That's definitely not my ringtone. Nick looked at me with disbelief in his eyes.

"Hello?" I picked up, my mouth suddenly dry.

"STELLA? STELLA GRAND?" A woman's voice blasted through the line, chaos and chattering echoing in the background.

"Uhh... yes?"

"Tell me, Nick is there. Err...Santa. Is he there? We finally managed to locate his sleigh."

I blinked. "Um... who is this?" It was a ridiculous question, but my mind was still comprehending the fact that I got a call from the North Pole.

"I'm Piper, head of operations from the North Pole. Please tell me he's there."

I stared at the phone. Then at Nick.

He mouthed: *Piper?? Oh God.*

"Um... yes. He's here." I managed to answer.

Nick winced. "Tell her I said hi."

Piper clearly heard him.

"Oh, he's ALIVE. Great. Wonderful. PUT HIM ON BEFORE I KILL HIM."

I slowly extended the phone to him.

"It's for you," I said flatly.

Nick swore under his breath and took the phone. "Pipes, hey girl."

I buried my face in my hands. God, he's such an asshole. The phone wasn't on speaker, but I could still hear Piper's voice loud and clear.

"NICK, IT'S CHRISTMAS EVE, WHERE THE FUCK ARE YOU?!"

Nick sucked in a breath. "Well, funny story, my sleigh crashed and..."

"Mm-hmm, great story, Nick, get back here now! We need to load the sleigh, and everyone is going crazy."

"Well, the thing is, the reindeer scattered and I need to find them too..."

"WHAT?!"

He yanked the phone away from his ear with a hiss.

"Get. Back. Seriously, Nick, you need to be back before Dusk, or Christmas gets cancelled."

"On it, Pipes."

He hung up slowly, rubbing the back of his neck.

I swallowed. "Soooo... that sounded... bad?"

"Well, it's not ideal." He rubbed the back of his head. "We need to catch Rudolf."

I nodded, even though the weight in my chest felt like it had doubled. "Let's get ready then."

But he didn't move. Instead, he looked at me, *really* looked at me.

"Wait... I don't want to," he said quietly, his voice cracked. "I just... I don't want to leave you."

My breath hitched. "I don't want you to go."

His eyes darkened. "Do you believe in soulmates?"

I laughed softly. "I didn't even believe in Santa Claus until three days ago."

"Now?" I looked up at him. The man who'd crashed into my roof, ruined my routine, and turned my world into magic.

"Now," I said, "I think I'd be stupid not to believe in *you.*"

He kissed me, gentle and lingering. "Stella....I..."

"Don't." I cut him off. "Don't make this harder."

He leaned back, biting his lips, then nodded. "Yes, you're right. Let's catch our reindeer."

Chapter 13
Nick
December 24

Dusk was falling fast, dragging long shadows through Everpine's streets like fingers trying to pull the day away before we were ready.

The map flickered again. One second, Rudolph was half a block away. Next, he was gone entirely.

I swore. Loudly. And for five minutes straight.

"Do they not know it's Christmas?" I growled, gripping the edge of the hot cocoa stand like it had personally betrayed me.

Stella's hand touched my shoulder, light and grounding. "Maybe they're just mad you keep shouting their names in public like a maniac."

Normally, I'd throw a line back. Tease her. But the weight of the ticking clock was settling between my ribs like ice. I shook my head.

"We're running out of time," I said, and this time, I couldn't keep the fear out of my voice.

She didn't have a comeback. No sass. No sarcasm. Just her fingers slipping into mine.

I looked at her, and I swear, I almost said it. Right then. Right there. But the words caught in my throat, strangled by the very fact that I'd have to leave. So instead, I held her hand tighter. Hoping she'd understand what I couldn't say.

The market was thinning out around us, vendors packing up, and lights dimming. The magic of Christmas Eve was still there, soft and quiet, like the hush of freshly fallen snow. But it felt... different. Like the end of something, not the beginning.

From inside a candle shop, old music played, the scratchy vinyl version of *Have Yourself a Merry Little Christmas*. Lights blinked from the lampposts like they were struggling to stay awake. My breath curled in the cold air, and I felt Stella's hand tremble just a little in mine.

I ran my thumb in slow circles over her knuckles, just to remind us both that we were still here. Still holding on.

Every step we took felt heavier. Like the road was ending beneath our feet.

And then...

"Wait," I said, stopping short.

Stella jerked toward me. "What? What is it?"

I pointed, my breath catching. In the center of the town square, under the enormous, glittering Christmas tree, stood Rudolph. No glow. Just standing there, blinking like he'd been waiting hours for us to catch up.

I narrowed my eyes. "He's waiting."

Stella whispered, "For what?"

I didn't take my eyes off him. "For me."

I let go of her hand and stepped forward slowly, like I was approaching a skittish god. The air shimmered faintly around him, static, magic, or both.

Rudolph didn't move. Just stood there with the kind of judgment only a centuries-old reindeer could muster.

I stopped five feet away.

"You done being dramatic?" I asked.

He blinked.

"Look," I said. "I get it. Everything exploded. You were scared. The others bolted. You've got every right to be pissed."

He huffed, but didn't budge.

"You're the heart of the sleigh and you know it," I continued.

Still nothing.

I exhaled hard. "Fine. I'll say it. I was an asshole. I took the sleigh out when I shouldn't have. Got cocky. Got lazy."

Rudolph's ears flicked.

"But..." My voice dropped. "Something good came out of it."

I turned my head toward Stella. She looked like she was holding her breath.

"I met her," I said, soft but clear. "And for that... I'm not sorry."

Rudolph blinked once. Twice. Then...light.

A soft red shimmer flickered at the tip of his nose. Then brighter and brighter.

Until suddenly...*Crack.*

Magic rippled through the sky like sleigh bells shaking loose from the clouds.

Gold wind curled across the rooftops. Sparkles drifted through the air like snow dusted in starlight. And then...hoof beats.

Dancer. Vixen. Blitzen. Comet. Dasher. Cupid. Donner. Prancer.

They all stepped into the square, their magic syncing like a heartbeat. One by one, they came to stand behind Rudolph, forming a perfect V.

The sleigh was ready. The sky buzzed with restored magic. It tugged at my bones. Called me home.

I looked up.

"I can go back," I said.

But the words tasted wrong. Stella was still beside me, eyes wide, lips parted, like she couldn't believe what she was seeing.

"So..." she said quietly, "that's it?"

I looked at her.

God, I wanted to kiss her.

I wanted to grab her hand and take her with me. But that wasn't how it worked.

"Not yet," I said.

Chapter 14
Stella
December 24

We walked back to the bakery. The reindeer, finally, fully reunited, were lined up behind the bakery in the back lot. Nick stood near the hearth, dressed in full Santa mode now, which for him meant a red sweater, black jeans, and a red beanie.

And he was getting ready to leave.

"This is it, huh?" I asked, trying to keep my voice light, teasing.

"Stella..." he stepped closer, brushing his thumb along my cheek like he was memorizing the shape of me. His eyes were so soft it hurt.

"Soulmates are real," he said quietly. "Just like me."

My breath snagged.

"All these years," he went on, "even I wasn't sure. I never felt this for anyone. I thought I was fine with flirting and meaningless hookups, but the truth is..." he swallowed, voice cracking. "I was lonely. And miserable..."

It felt like all the air was trapped inside me or all the air was sucked out from earth as I listened to him, my heart aching with each word.

"... Until you."

The world tilted around me.

"You made me feel," he whispered. "In five days. Five days, Stella. You made me feel more than I have in centuries. You're my soulmate. I know it the same way I know Christmas magic is real."

I stared at him, wide-eyed, tears burning hot behind my lashes.

He took a step forward. "Say something."

I didn't. I just launched myself at him, wrapping my arms around his neck, kissing him hard, like I could pour every fear, every want, and every broken wish into that one last kiss.

His hands found my waist, lifted me clean off the ground. My legs wrapped around him on instinct, ankles crossing at the small of his back.

"Nick," I breathed against his mouth, forehead pressed to his. "I want you. One last time. Please."

In response, he deepened the kiss. His arms tightened around my waist, and he walked us backward through the doorway, kicking the door shut behind us with his heel.

In a few seconds, we shed all our clothes. My fingers traced his muscles while he showered me with kisses. The cold air hit my bare skin, and then his heat chased it away, mouth and hands everywhere at once.

I followed the hard lines of him: the slope of his shoulders, the ridges of his abs, the faint scar just under his left pec. He shuddered under my touch, breath hitching when I dragged my nails down his back.

Every kiss felt like a promise and a goodbye. When he closed his mouth over my nipple, I cried out, fingers twisting in his curls. He moved lower, mapping my ribs, my stomach, and the soft skin just above my hipbone that made my thighs fall open without permission.

He positioned himself at my entrance, making my back arch from the sensation. One slow, perfect thrust, and he was home. We both stilled, gasping at the overwhelming rightness of it. Then he moved, deep and steady, like he was trying to rewrite time itself. I wrapped my legs high around his waist, heels digging into the small of his back, urging him deeper.

"Look at me, baby."

I did, the fire burning in me, and pleasure coursing hot through my veins.

"I want you, Nick," I panted, nails raking down his spine. "I want you everywhere. Claim me. Every inch. So even when you're gone, my body remembers it's yours."

His eyes flashed dark and dangerous. He slowed, just enough to make me whine, then dragged his thumb through the slick mess between us.

"You want this?" He murmured in a low and sultry voice.

I nodded frantically, a broken sound catching in my throat as the pad of his thumb pressed inside. Just a tease. Just enough to make my hips jerk.

"Yes...God, yes..."

He worked his way slowly and deliberately, kept thrusting in me until the pressure low inside my spine detonated and I shattered around his cock.

My body was still convulsing when he pushed his tip between my cheeks. My eyes rolled back as his thumb grazed over my clit. He drove in, slow, relentless, swallowing every whimper with his mouth on mine. The stretch was impossible, too much and not enough at the same time. When he bottomed out, we both groaned, foreheads pressed together, trembling.

"Fuck, Stella." He growled, trembling above me.

"Give me more," I whimpered, nails digging into his shoulders. "Give me everything, Nick. I need it. Need you."

His thrust unraveled me. His hand slid between us, middle finger slipping into my soaked heat alongside where we were already joined, his thumb finding my clit with merciless precision. The sudden fullness ripped a scream from me.

"Nick...oh God..."

"That's it," he rasped, voice shredded. "Take it all. Every fucking inch."

"Come for me one more time," he growled against my lips. "Come while I'm in every part of you."

I couldn't speak, couldn't think. Just felt. The thick drag of him in my ass, his finger curling inside me, thumb circling, circling, until my entire body was one live wire. Pleasure coiled vicious and tight, then snapped.

The orgasm tore through me like wildfire, back bowing off the bed, vision whiting out behind clenched eyelids. I screamed his name, walls fluttering around his finger, clenching down so hard he cursed and faltered. But he didn't stop. Kept thrusting, kept stroking, and riding me through it until another wave crashed over me without warning, smaller but sharper, ripping a sob from my throat.

"Nick, Nick...I can't..."

"You can," he panted, sweat dripping from his jaw onto my chest. "You're doing it. You're perfect. Such a good girl."

The praise snapped something inside me. I came again, my arousal gushed down my thighs. His rhythm stuttered, hips slamming deep one last time before he spilled with a guttural moan. Hot ropes of cum flooded me.

We collapsed in a tangle of sweat and limbs. He stayed buried deep, arms shaking as he held me close, lips brushing my temple, my eyelids, the tears tracking into my hair.

"I've got you," he whispered, voice hoarse and reverent. "I've got you, baby."

I couldn't answer. Could only cling to him, legs wrapped tight, body still pulsing around him in lazy aftershocks.

Outside, the reindeer stamped one final time. The clock on the wall ticked past five. He kissed me slowly and deeply.

When he finally pulled out, we both winced. He tucked me against his chest, fingers combing through my hair.

"I have to go." His voice shook, and his eyes were gleaming.

"I know." Tears ran down my cheeks. "But I don't want to watch you go."

He pressed a soft kiss on the top of my head. "Then don't."

I managed to nod, he quickly dressed up, and shot me one last look from the doorway.

"Bye, Sweetheart."

"Bye, Santa."

Chapter 15
Stella
One year later - December 25

Everpine hadn't changed one bit. It still looked like a Pinterest board, something tourists loved, of course. The main square was crowded with people trying to get a picture with a giant inflatable snowman. Carolers could be found at every corner, and Christmas music played from everywhere, until I was able to memorize each and every line.

Last year, on Christmas morning, I woke up to find my roof fixed and the interior looking better than ever. That was the last sign of him.

Business had been blooming. Everyone kept asking where the handsome man from last year was, and with a tight smile, I always answered. "He's out of town."

I decided to sleep in on Christmas morning. The last month was a crazy mess covered in frosting and flour. Christmas this year didn't feel the same. I still worked, but I allowed myself to stop and enjoy the small moments. I even visited Boston for the first time since I left, and everything felt oddly... comforting.

But still, the memory of him lingered, and with every fiber of my being, I hoped he showed up, crashing into my roof again.

But he didn't.

There was so much I wanted to tell him. After he left, I wanted to get back to my quiet life, but a nudge in my chest kept poking out.

I loved him. I didn't know how it happened, but he was right. Soulmates do exist, and he was mine.

It sounded ridiculous, even in my head, to say that Santa Claus is my soulmate, but that was the truth. I fell in love with this smug asshole, and before I could say something to him, he left.

I brewed some coffee and wrapped a blanket around myself. The snow was falling outside like powdered sugar, and the streets felt calm. You could hear children's laughter echo like it was true magic.

Jingle.

Huh?

I hurried towards my backyard, my heart pounding. He was there. Standing in the snow, hands in his pockets, with a wicked grin on his face.

"Hey, Sweetheart."

My breath caught, and my legs moved on their own. I ran towards him and he waited for me with open arms. Lifting me easily, I wrapped my legs around his waist; his mouth found mine easily.

The taste of him hit me, sweetness gliding down my throat. Our tongues tangled together in a frantic rhythm.

When we finally pulled apart, I was gasping. "How... Why...?"

He brushed my hair back and held me tighter. "It took a while to figure out. I didn't want to come back until I was sure I could stay."

I blinked, my breath caught in my throat. "S-stay?"

His smirk widened. "Yes, Sweetheart."

He set me down and gestured toward the small, unused shed at the edge of the yard. "I hope you won't be mad that I borrowed this without permission."

I blinked, dazed. "You what?"

He pushed the door open, and my jaw hit the floor. My tiny shed was expanded inside, workshop tables everywhere, and elves running around with boxes.

"You... What... is this?" I stuttered, my mind working in overdrive mode.

"I figured your backyard was as good a place as any for a North Pole annex."

"You brought the North Pole *here*?"

"Not all of it. Just part. I'll still have to go back sometimes, but I'm not bound to the place anymore."

He stepped closer, voice quiet. "I can live here. With you. If you'll have me."

I stared at him. Heart in my throat.

"You want to live *here*? In *Everpine*?"

"I want to live with you."

Tears hit before I could stop them.

"I love you," I whispered.

He slipped his hand to the back of my neck and pulled me close to him. "I love you so much, Sweetheart."

He leaned in and kissed me, slow, arms around my waist.

Then, against my lips, he murmured, "What do you say I let the elves finish unpacking, and I show you just how much I love you?"

My thighs clenched at the promise in his voice.

I grinned. "Sounds like an amazing idea... Santa."

Epilogue

Stella
December 31

I never thought I would spend New Year's Eve coming on Santa's cock, but here we are.

Everpine had two moods: festive and aggressively festive. Twinkle lights sparkled down every storefront. Fireworks were already being set up along the lake. And my bakery? We were selling champagne macaroons and champagne *with* macaroons. I was on my third flute, which was not ideal considering I had to operate a bakery.

Nick had vanished earlier in the day for "one last delivery run." I didn't ask questions. But as the hours ticked closer to midnight, I started to worry he might not make it back in time.

But one hour before midnight, I heard it.

A familiar jingle.

The sleigh landed behind my bakery with a soft *thud* in the snow. And there he was, Nick, in all his cocky, broad-shouldered glory.

"Hey, Sweetheart." He welcomed me when I stepped outside.

"I was beginning to think you bailed on me."

"Never, baby." He offered his hand. "Get in the sleigh."

"What?"

"We're going for a ride." His smirk deepened. "And I've got you a late Christmas present."

Inside the sleigh, he handed me a perfectly wrapped box with a red satin bow. I opened it, and my cheeks flushed instantly.

Inside was a red lace bodysuit, obscenely sheer, with a crotchless slit and matching red velvet cuffs.

"Get changed, baby," he whispered, low and dark.

Inside the sleigh, it was surprisingly warm. Nick went to check on the reindeer, and I slipped into the lace suit.

When he came back, his eyes darkened, devouring me already, making me clench my thighs.

"Let's go, boys." He snapped the reins, and we took off. The sleigh lurched skyward with a rush of cold that kissed every inch of bare skin the lace left exposed.

Everpine's lights glittered around us, and Nick's body pressed down on mine, his warmth seeping into me. He shed his clothes, and his hands cupped my breast, hard enough to bruise.

Thumbs flicked my nipples through the sheer fabric until they throbbed in time with the sleigh's rhythm.

His fingers dipped lower, and I was drenched. They slid deep, curling, stroking that spot that made my back bow against his chest.

"Fuck, baby," he rasped, his breath was hot on my neck. "You're dripping down my wrist."

I couldn't answer. Could only whimper as he finger-fucked me in long, lazy strokes while the sleigh leveled out above the clouds. Stars wheeled overhead, sharp as broken glass. Far below, the first test firework popped.

He pulled his fingers free and brought them to my lips. "Taste yourself. Taste what Santa does to good girls who wait up."

I sucked them clean, and his groan vibrated through my body.

"Such a good girl," he murmured. "Put your hands above your head."

My body reacted to him instantly. The cuffs clicked, binding me to the sleigh. The short chain forced my arms overhead, breasts thrust forward, body arched like a bow. The position yanked the lace tight across my nipples and left my slick, open pussy tilted toward the sky.

He lowered himself, his beard scraped against my inner thigh, and I felt deliciously helpless. His mouth suddenly sealed over me, coaxing a loud moan from me.

He licked one long, slow stripe from clit to entrance, groaning like a man tasting heaven. The sound vibrated straight through my core. His tongue plunged inside, fucking me in shallow, greedy thrusts while his nose nudged my clit. I jerked against the cuffs, the chain rattled like sleigh bells, sharp and sweet.

He pulled back just enough to suck my clit between his lips, hard, relentless suction that made my vision spark white. Two fingers replaced his tongue, curling deep, scissoring, and stretching me open while he flicked and fluttered and ruined me with that wicked mouth.

He added a third finger, stretching me wide, and curled them hard against that spot that made my thighs quake. At the same time, he grazed my clit with his teeth, and I shattered.

The orgasm slammed through me like a blizzard, sudden and blinding. I screamed into the air, walls clamping around his fingers in violent pulses, my arousal flooding his tongue. He didn't stop. He licked me through every aftershock, gentler now, savoring, until I sagged in the restraints, trembling and oversensitive.

He undid my cuffs, my arms dropped, clinging to his neck, and he bottomed out in one brutal thrust. My back arched against the sky, my swollen clit throbbed against his pelvis. He set a brutal rhythm, hips snapping, balls slapping my clit with every thrust. One hand fisted in my hair, arching my neck back.

Somewhere in the distance, I could hear bells ringing. It was midnight, and fireworks exploded around us.

I was already close again, impossibly, embarrassingly close. He felt it, the way I fluttered around him, and laughed low against my ear.

"Come on Santa's cock, Stella. Right fucking now."

He reached down and pinched my clit hard, and I detonated. I milked him in endless spasms. He followed with a guttural roar, hips stuttering as he spilled hot and thick inside me, pulse after pulse until it leaked down my thighs in the rushing wind.

He flipped us over so that I was straddling him, still buried deep inside me, and we just sagged together. As the fireworks continued to explode, people cheered and celebrated.

"Happy New Year, Sweetheart," he whispered, brushing a soft kiss on my lips.

"Happy New Year, Santa." I breathed. "Best New Year's Eve ever."

His cock twitched inside me, already stirring again.

"Night's young," he said with a smirk. "Let's see how many times I can make you come until we land."

Author note

Thank you so much for reading Santa, Baby!

It would mean the world to me if you left a review or a rating, so I can continue improving my writing.

Please note that English is my second language, so if you notice any grammatical issues, feel free to let me know!

Stalk me on my socials:

TikTok: Linda Evermill

Insta: Linda Evermill

Make sure to check out the first book in the Aresix trilogy, which is a spicy post-apocalyptic romance:

In the Shadow of the Virus

Acknowledgements

Okay, so truth be told, this book wasn't planned. I was knee-deep in writing book two of the Aresix series when I saw a TikTok that just inspired me, and I had to bring Nick and Stella's story to life.

Huge thanks to my fiancée, who patiently listened to my rambles about Santa's dick.

I'm so grateful for all my beta and ARC readers. Without you guys, I would be lost.

Special thanks and shout-out to Amanda. I want to let everyone know that, from now on, every book I write is for her. :D

But in all seriousness, thank you, love, for everything. I'm so glad that I've met you, and we're keeping our flame baby alive.

About the Author

Linda Evermill (formerly publishing as Lidum) writes spicy, addictive romance filled with emotional depth, tension, and a touch of darkness.

She is the author *of In the Shadow of the Virus* and *Santa, Baby*, and her upcoming release, *In the Darkness of the Guilt*, continues her signature blend of heat and heart across multiple romance subgenres.

Linda loves crafting stories with passion, vulnerability, and complicated relationships, whether the vibe is dark and gritty or playful and festive.

When she's not writing, she's usually binge-watching TV shows, growing her never-ending TBR pile, and devouring smutty little books for "research."

Printed in Dunstable, United Kingdom